WILD CHILD

TAMSIN LEY

with

AURORA SHIFTERS

TWIN LEAF PRESS

All characters in this book, be they supernatural, human, or something else entirely, are the product of the author's imagination. Any resemblance to actual people, situations, or events are entirely coincidental.

No part of this book may be reproduced, transmitted, or distributed in any form or by any means without explicit written permission from the author, with the exception of brief quotes for use in reviews, articles, or blogs. This book is licensed for your enjoyment only. Thank you a million zillion hearts and kisses for purchasing.

Paperback version
ISBN-13: 978-1-950027-37-8
Copyright © 2021 Twin Leaf Press

Ash pulled his ski hat down over his forehead to block the bitter wind coming in off the inlet. Downtown Anchorage in February could feel like the North Pole, despite the sun hitting the dirty snow lining the street. Even his inner wolf was curled up in a ball, content to avoid being called on to do anything in this frigid weather. Pink sidewalk salt crunched under Ash's boots as he skirted a cart selling reindeer sausage. The Fur Rendezvous festival was gearing up, and despite the temperature, the sidewalks teemed with people.

He'd gotten word that the heiress he was tracking had been selling of her jewelry at a pawn shop nearby, and the bounty on her was big—twenty-five thousand plus expenses. The reward would be enough to make a sizable dent in what he owed the pack. But only if he caught up to her before the other bounty hunters.

He waited for traffic to pass so he could cross the street, listening to the music from the carnival a few blocks down. Ahead, the wrought iron bars over the pawn shop windows glittered with frost, reminiscent of the cheap bling Ash knew was inside. The equally frosty glass obscured a mishmash of objects displayed for sale inside. A familiar, wiry figure stepped out of the shop, looked both directions, then locked eyes with Ash. *Damn it*. Talvin, a fox shifter from Bootlegger's Cove. Usually, he made his living serving papers for one of the local attorneys, but had also been known to pull in a bounty or two.

Ash darted across the street in front of a Suburban, ignoring the angry horn blast. He had to find out what Talvin had discovered before the man disappeared into the crowd. Skidding to a stop on the sidewalk, Ash planted one hand against the side of the building to stop Talvin from rounding the corner.

Talvin cringed, zipping his worn coat up to his throat. "Hey, Ash. What's up?"

The guy knew why he was here, and Ash was in no mood for small talk. "What'd you find out?"

"Hey, I'm just shopping." The smaller man took a step back. "I don't want no trouble."

Ash ran his tongue along his front teeth and forced himself to calm down, conscious of a woman in a bulky parka covered with Fur Rendezvous pins passing behind him on the sidewalk. The last thing he needed was for someone to call the police. He was on APD's shit list, and they'd haul him in and ask questions later. Then he'd lose this bounty for sure.

Making his voice as calm as possible, he asked, "What'd you buy?"

Talvin pulled a phone out of his pocket. "New phone, man. Can I go?"

Chest tight, Ash lowered his arm, calling on his wolf's senses to take in the other shifter's scent as Talvin darted away. If he needed to, he could track the fox down after talking to the clerk inside the store. He waited until Talvin disappeared around the corner before pushing open the pawn shop door.

A door chime played an off-key rendition of Jingle Bells as he stepped into the scent of dust and old machine grease. He allowed his eyes a moment to adjust to the dim interior, noting the old theater curtain masking the back portion of the store as he tucked his gloves into his pocket. In the main area, odds and ends stacked the walls from ceiling to floor, everything from used bicycles and camping gear to toys and even a beat-up mannequin in a lavishly beaded wedding gown. Immediately to his left, a balding clerk with glasses sat on a stool between two glass-topped counters packed with guns and jewelry.

The man laid a tattered Louis L'Amour paperback face down on the counter behind him and pushed his glasses up his nose. "Buying or selling?"

Ash pulled a picture from his pocket. The woman he was tracking was from a red wolf pack down south, a pretty girl with a rounded face, plump lips, and long brown hair. Exactly Ash's type, though he couldn't concern himself with that. She wasn't smiling at the camera, but there was a glint in her eye that told him there was more to her than just her pretty looks. He held the photo out. "I'm looking for this woman. She been around here lately?"

The guy looked up at the stained acoustic ceiling tiles with a sigh. "God damn it. You're the second guy asking about her today. Is the stuff she's been selling me hot?"

"I wouldn't know," Ash said, pocketing the photo. *Should've known Talvin was lying.* He'd take care of that later. Right now, he needed to see what the clerk could tell him. "Her family hired me to find her. Any of the stuff she sold you still here?" If he could pick up a fresh scent, his wolf might be able to track her.

The clerk slid open the back of the glass counter and pulled out a diamond tennis bracelet. Even in the crappy florescent light, the diamonds glittered luxuriously. The piece had to be worth at least eight grand. "She brought this in last week. Not sure how I'm going to sell it, but I got it for a steal."

Ash reached for it, but the clerk pulled back, eying the tattoos on Ash's hand. "Look, no touch."

Staring the man down, Ash asked, "How am I supposed to judge if it's real?" It was, of course. The woman was an heiress, after all. But Ash wasn't interested in whether or not it was real. He just needed a good sniff.

The guy hesitated a moment, as if considering, then slowly extended his arm. "All right. Just know I have a gun if you do anything funky."

"I don't doubt that you do." Ash nodded respectfully and took the bracelet, pretending to examine the gems as he inhaled. The clerk's scent was topmost, a lingering odor of ham sandwich and beer. But there was another fragrance underneath, something that reminded him of rich velvet and chocolate.

Ash's wolf perked up. *Mate.*

Stand down, buddy. It had been a long time since Ash had been with a woman, but mates were rare, and the scent was too faint to jump to a rash conclusion like that. *Once we bag this bounty, we'll go out and celebrate.*

Handing the bracelet back to the clerk, Ash asked, "Anyone else look at this recently?"

The man's face lit up. "You interested? I'll give you an excellent deal."

"No. I asked if anyone else had looked at this." Luxuries were the last thing on Ash's mind. He needed to finish this job and pay off his debt. "What about that guy who was in here before me?"

The clerk scowled and shoved the bracelet back into the case beside the other bits of jewelry displayed on a black velvet tray. "Like I told him, I'm not in the information business. If you're not interested in buying, please leave."

Sighing, Ash dug in his pocket for his wallet. He pulled out his last twenty and placed it on the counter. "All I wanna know is if you know where that girl lives and if that fellow who was in here before me looked at any of her stuff."

The clerk crossed his arms and eyed the twenty before giving Ash a meaningful look.

"That's all I have," Ash said truthfully. Other than the punch card for a local deli, his wallet was empty. Then he added, "She's in danger," he added. People always wanted to protect a pretty girl.

Pushing his glasses up his nose, the man shrugged, then snaked his hand out and swept the twenty off the counter and into his pocket. "She told me she likes the Chinese place down the street. I think she also mentioned something about her condo being in walking distance."

"Thanks."

Ash headed out the door, his wolf pushing to get out and follow the woman's scent. There were only a couple of condo developments nearby; picking up her scent should be a cakewalk.

He was going to bag himself an heiress.

CHAPTER TWO

"No, no, no!" Melody bumped her car crookedly against the curb as the engine sputtered and died. The check engine light had been on for a week, but she didn't have the money to get it fixed. She stared at the gauges on the dash, the heater blowing tepid air at full blast against the frost-rimmed windshield. *Now what?*

Taking a deep breath, she turned the car off, waited a second, and tried to start it again. The blower resumed, but the engine refused to turn over. Closing her eyes, she fought back tears. A mere six months ago, she'd have called for a taxi and let AAA handle the rest. But she didn't even have insurance right now, let alone roadside assistance.

"Be strong, Melody. The condo is only a few blocks away," she told herself. Her food was definitely going to be cold by the time she got home.

The inside of the car smelled of sesame chicken—Chinese food was one of the few things that smelled good since getting pregnant. She'd lost her job as a barista after only a few days because the scent of coffee made her vomit, and she had to retreat to the bathroom every ten minutes. Every other place she'd applied wanted references, and she couldn't risk leaving a trail; Brennan, the pack Alpha, had connections and wouldn't rest until he found her.

Until she could find another job, she'd been forced to rely on pawning her jewelry to pay rent. The bracelet she'd sold last week should've fetched four times the price she'd gotten, but she was a terrible negotiator. She had no idea how she was going to last until the baby was born, let alone take care of it afterward.

Now her car was kaput. She had to come up with a plan, fast, or she'd be forced to go back to her pack with her proverbial tail between her legs. She could picture the scar on Brennan's upper lip curling in pleasure as he deliberated on how to punish her for running away.

Baby fluttered against her bladder, a new sensation over the last week, reminding her of another urgent need; she had to pee. "All right, all right, I'm going," she said, picking up the loops of the white plastic bag with her food.

She stepped out of the car onto the icy curb and zipped her parka over her gently swelling belly, though it did little against the icy wind. Her cheeks were already numb. Adjusting her scarf up around her throat, she dug in her purse for some change for the meter.

A passing man in a wool dress coat said, "That's a handicapped spot, in case you didn't notice."

Her shoulders sagged. He was right. She closed her purse and turned away. "Guess that's one way to get a free tow."

That got her a look from two women in designer ski parkas, so she clamped her mouth closed. Mom used to berate her for thinking out loud, but she couldn't seem to stop herself. Not even after Brennan gave her a bloody lip for speaking her mind.

Putting her back to the wind, she began trudging down the sidewalk toward home. A local festival was in full swing, filling the air with carnival music and laughter, and pedestrians hunched inside their parkas as they hurried along the sidewalks.

She turned the corner toward her condo. It was in a crappy district, but hadn't required references, and it had a spectacular view of Mt. Susitna. The Sleeping Lady, as the locals called it, reminded her of a pregnant woman, a comrade she often sat and talked to while alone in her living room. And since her escape from the pack, she was alone a lot.

"Better alone than in bad company," she said toward her belly.

The street sloped downward toward the industrial section of town and a bustling parking lot full of carnival rides. The building superintendent didn't seem to think the sidewalk along the street was part of his jurisdiction, so the path wasn't salted. Melody's designer boots had no traction on the ice, and she had to grip the fence rail for balance as she moved toward the side doorway. One block down, near the flashing lights of the carnival, what appeared to be a small child in a green snowsuit sailed into the air, arms flailing.

Melody paused, gaping. "What's going on?"

The crowd cheered, and the child seemed to cartwheel upward again.

If she hadn't been so cold, she might've continued past her condo to check things out, but the wind was driving daggers into her exposed cheeks. She rounded the gate post and headed toward the building. Maybe she'd be able to see the activity from her window.

Fingers stiff, she fumbled in her pocket for her keys before noticing that someone had left the door ajar—again. "Oh, no."

She stepped inside and pulled the door firmly closed behind her, glancing around for signs of an intruder. Last time, a homeless guy had fallen asleep in the elevator and she'd been forced to use the stairs. Her place was on the third floor, and right now, her feet were numb. She pushed the elevator button. "Please be empty."

Thankfully, it was. The jerky ride to her floor reminded her she had to pee, and she raced to her front door. Dropping her now-cold food on the arm of the sofa, she locked the door behind her, then stripped out of her parka as she beelined it across the tiny living area, through her bedroom, and into the bathroom.

"Gotta pee, gotta pee, gotta pee," she chanted as she hurried to get her pants down. She was so chilly, even the hard toilet seat felt warm against her skin. Blessed relief filled her as she emptied her bladder.

She was washing her hands when she heard a creak, like someone was moving around her bedroom. Turning off the water, she stood still and listened.

Another floorboard popped.

Every muscle in her body tensed. Although she'd been born to shifter parents, she didn't have a shifter form to protect herself. Grandfather said mom had given her weak genes. *I should call the police.* Except her phone was in her coat pocket near the front door.

Breathing hard, she looked for something to use as a weapon. The only item in reach was the toilet brush, so she grabbed it and peered into the murky twilight of her bedroom. The blinds were shut, but there was enough light to see the bedcovers were rumpled, just as she'd left them. The closet didn't have any doors for someone to hide behind. Maybe she'd imagined it. The building *was* old and creaky.

Heart thundering, she crept into the room. The top drawer of her dresser hung open. Had she left it that way? The last of her jewelry was in that drawer, her only hope of staying afloat until after the baby was born and she could land another job. She grew light-headed. What if he'd already been in here when she got home and she hadn't noticed? The thief could be escaping right now.

Still wielding the toilet brush, she rushed toward the drawer and peered inside. She'd never been one for folding clothes, and her panties and bras lay jumbled inside. She gingerly nudged the lingerie aside, looking for the silk pouch with her jewelry.

It wasn't there.

"Mother fucker," she said out loud, anger displacing her fear.

She pivoted to the door. If the thief was still in the house, she was going to at least get a description to help the police catch the crook. How dare someone break in here and touch her things? She burst out of her bedroom into the small living area and collided against something solid. Huge. *And living.*

A giant, tattooed man stood between her and the exit.

Ash threw out his arms to keep Melody from toppling backward as she rebounded off his chest. She was wielding a toilet brush like a cudgel and reeled backward a few steps, her lips forming a lush circle of surprise. She was even more stunning in person than in her picture, and now that he had her face-to-face, Ash could no longer deny what his wolf had been telling him since the moment he detected her scent on the bracelet.

Melody Rush was his mate.

"Shit." He sighed. Could fate be more cruel? The woman he was supposed to capture was also the one he was destined to protect, honor, and cherish.

"The police are on their way," she said through bared teeth.

Protect her, his wolf urged.

His gaze fell to the gentle mound of her stomach. The intel hadn't included that she was pregnant, but his wolf senses confirmed what his eyes were seeing. As a rule, he never asked why someone was paying him to find someone—better to not know, especially on some of his shadier jobs. But her family was obviously worried if they were willing to pay to bring her home safely. He smiled. *I can both protect her and collect this bounty.*

"Take a breath." He stepped forward, waiting for her to catch his scent. To sense their mate bond.

She took another step back. "Give me back my jewelry, and I'll consider letting you go."

He paused and narrowed his eyes in confusion. Why didn't she acknowledge the mate bond? Perhaps the pregnancy hormones were keeping her wolf more subdued than usual; he couldn't detect it at the moment. He took another step forward. "I don't have your jewelry."

"I mean it. Empty your pockets." This time she held her ground, sweeping the toilet brush in front of her like a rapier.

He lifted his hands to show they were empty. "Or what? You'll scrub me to death?"

"Please, just put it all back." Her voice shook. "I need it to survive. The baby needs it."

Her desperation brought to mind another woman, a woman begging him not to make her obey, not to make her betray the man she loved. He clamped down on the memory. But it made him wonder if Melody could be refusing to acknowledge the mate bond because she was committed to the baby's father. If that was the case, he needed to find out more before pushing forward.

He stopped his advance. "Your family sent me."

She made a choking noise and stumbled backward. "You're a… a bounty hunter?"

"Take a breath." His wolf was pacing inside him. Howling. Aching to be acknowledged. "Don't you recognize me?"

"I don't care who you are. Get the hell out of my house."

The way her chest was heaving, he was worried she was going to hyperventilate, and there was zero recognition in her eyes. If she couldn't detect the mate bond by smell, there was only one other way he could think of to show her.

In two swift strides, he yanked the toilet brush from her grip and tossed it away. Pulling her close, he clamped his lips over hers, covering her gasp of surprise. She tasted just as he expected, lush with a hint of sweetness, like chocolate melting against his tongue. He prodded between her lips, seeking entry, seeking a way to connect with her.

But instead of returning his kiss, she bit down. Hard. He tasted blood and pulled back in surprise.

Then she screamed. A full-out, terrified, high-pitched scream. Her hands beat against his chest as she wriggled to escape his grasp. "Let me go! Help! Help!"

Fuck. Kissing her had been a huge mistake. She was still clueless about the mate bond, and now probably thought he was a rapist. "I shouldn't have done that. I'm sorry."

Still screaming, she attempted to knee him in the groin, but he twisted and caught the blow against his thigh.

"Hush." He clamped a hand over her mouth. "The neighbors are going to call the police."

She tried to bite him again.

Fierce little vixen. He liked a woman who wouldn't roll over and give up. But right now, he couldn't afford to put up with her resistance. She might not recognize him as her mate—yet—but he could still move forward on the bounty.

"I'm not going to hurt you," he said. "I just want to talk. Promise no more screaming?"

Glaring into his eyes, she nodded, and he slowly released his hand from her mouth.

She spit in his face, velvet brown eyes flashing. "How dare you try to kiss me! Does my family know the sort of man they hired? Brennan will have your hide when he finds out."

"Brennan?" The name didn't ring a bell.

"My fiancé, you asshole." She shoved against his chest, trying to free herself. "The pack Alpha."

The more he heard, the less he liked. This contract was more complicated than a family worrying about a pregnant daughter. Melody had apparently hitched herself to an Alpha, which had all sorts of implications. He set her on her feet and stepped back, letting his gaze slide down her front to her abdomen. "I take it the baby's his?"

Going rigid, she said, "The baby is mine."

He pressed his tongue against the back of his teeth, wondering if this Brennan guy even knew she was pregnant. Was the baby his and he wanted it back? Or perhaps she'd run away because the baby *wasn't* Brennan's and she was afraid of being punished. Ash didn't give a shit one way or the other. She was his mate, and he would protect her, bounty be damned.

"I can keep you safe," he said, keeping his voice even. "Just tell me what's going on."

She shook her head. "It's better if you pretend you were never here. If Brennan finds out you kissed his fiancé, he'll rip your bowels out through your mouth. I've seen him do it. Let me go, and I won't tell."

Things clicked into place. *Is she trying to protect* me? Maybe that's why she wasn't acknowledging the mate bond.

"Nope." He bent and retrieved her coat from the floor. He was done playing around. He'd worry about the bounty later. Right now he needed to get her out of here and somewhere safe, where they could figure things out. "Get your things. You're coming with me. Now."

She glanced between him and the door, as if contemplating escape.

He raised his eyebrows and shrugged. "Don't need anything? Okay, then let's go."

"No, wait!" She clenched her fists in helpless frustration. "Fine, I'll come. But at least give me back my jewelry."

"I didn't take your stuff. Go check your drawer again."

Her brows furrowed into a glower. "So you did go through my things."

Heat crept up his neck as he realized she now knew he'd been poking through her underwear drawer. Even though his human side had been in denial about Melody being his mate, he hadn't been able to stop his wolf's curiosity while he'd waited for her to return. The girl had taste, and he'd enjoyed a brief fantasy of ripping the lacy bits of cloth off her curves.

Shaking off the thoughts, he said, "Just pack a bag and let's go. There's another bounty hunter on your trail."

"Who cares?" She rolled her eyes but at least turned to the bedroom. "My life is over no matter who takes me in."

He didn't know why she said that, but there wasn't time to find out. Talvin could show up at any time, and Ash was going to keep her to himself until he figured out what was going on with the bounty—and their mate bond.

Melody couldn't help but feel embarrassed as she located the bag with her jewelry still buried in a back corner of her dresser, just as the man now blocking her bedroom doorway had said. Stuffing the silk pouch in her purse, she started throwing clothes into her suitcase. There was no choice but to go with the bounty hunter, at least for now. Part of her hoped she'd find an opportunity to make a run for it, but in her heart she knew there would not be another escape. Brennan had found her. Her only shot at freedom was gone.

The moment she latched her suitcase closed, the bounty hunter was ready with her coat, holding it up to help her into it. Maybe he was trying to make up for forcing the kiss on her earlier, or keep her from ratting him out to Brennan. She had no intention of telling that Alpha bastard anything, but she didn't want the bounty hunter to know that. Better to keep this guy on his best behavior. Besides, it was nice to be looked after, even if in the smallest of ways.

He lifted her suitcase as if it weighed nothing and guided her toward the door with a firm hand at her elbow.

As they waited for the elevator, her gaze roamed over the ink creeping up his neck out of the black Carhartt coat and flowing over the backs of his hands. She couldn't tell exactly what the designs were. Perhaps flames and leaves? How much of his broad shoulders and chest did the tattoos cover? She'd never been attracted to tattoos, yet found herself unable to look away.

"Name's Ash, by the way," he said as they stepped onto the elevator and he pushed the button for the ground floor.

"Ash what?" She figured she may as well know his name.

"Huntington."

The elevator bumped to a stop, and the door opened, letting them step into the hall on the main floor. He put a hand against her lower back, pushing her toward the glass double doors outside. "Huntington the bounty hunter." She huffed a mirthless laugh and pulled away from his touch. "How long have you been ruining people's lives?"

His mouth twitched as if he wanted to smile, but he didn't. "Pretty much since I was able." Darkness had fallen, and the snow kicked up by passing cars created a mist of glittering ice shards under the streetlamps. Ash sized up the thin parka stretched tight over her rounded middle. "Is that your only coat?"

"Yes." From the opposite side of the building, the noise of the carnival carried on, as if mocking her with unattainable freedom. "Where are we going?"

"I'm a couple of blocks over." He removed his parka and draped it around her shoulders.

Her body shuddered in pleasure from his residual body heat, and she wrapped it tighter around herself. The bounty hunter could freeze to death for all she cared. Yet he didn't seem to mind the cold. He wore a long-sleeved tee shirt, the muscles on his chest and arms bulging beneath the fabric, nipples forming tiny hard points under his shirt. Her gaze kept creeping sideways toward him, her thoughts going places they shouldn't. Did he have a lot of hair on his chest, or was he smooth? It was a strange thing to wonder, but she'd only been with Brennan, promised to him since she was eleven, and his body had been like a sheepskin rug.

Ash slowed, and she spotted the lumpy form of a homeless person wrapped in a sleeping bag hunched in a doorway ahead. She expected Ash to skirt the guy, but he directed them straight for the man.

Her chest tightened. Homeless people made her even more uncomfortable than tattooed bounty hunters.

Pulling a card from his pocket, Ash nudged the man with a foot.

Two bloodshot eyes peered at them above the edge of the sleeping bag. "I just got warm, man."

"Free sandwich." Ash set what looked like a punch card on top of the sleeping bag and kept moving.

"So you can be nice to him, but not to me?" she asked once they were out of earshot.

"He doesn't have a bounty on his head. Or much of anything, obviously. Besides, we're leaving town, and the card expires in a couple of days." He stopped at an old black pickup with a topper and put her suitcase in the back. After helping her settle onto the bench on the passenger side, he moved around to the driver's side.

Her eyes followed him, noticing his liquid grace. He didn't move with the stiffness of a musclebound man, and she wondered if he worked out or was just naturally fit. He might even be able to take Brennan in a fight—not that he would; he was going to cash her in like a poker chip and be done with her.

The truck started with a rumble, and Ash cranked the heater to full before pulling into traffic. Melody expected him to take them toward the airport, but instead he continued down the highway out of town.

"Um, where are we going?" she asked, looking at an enormous star outlined in lights on a mountaintop ahead.

"Birchwood Airport."

She raised her eyebrows. She'd only been here two months and knew little about the area north of the city other than it was separated by a military base. "I thought Anchorage was the only one."

"Nope."

She waited for him to elaborate, examining his face under the waxing and waning light from the street lamps along the highway. Strong jaw with a five o'clock shadow. Dark eyebrows. A nose that looked as if it'd been broken more than once. If she'd met him in a dark alley, she'd be terrified, but she felt strangely comfortable with him right now—probably because he couldn't collect the bounty if she was hurt.

When it became apparent he wasn't going to say anything else about the airport, she asked, "How did you find me, anyway?"

He shrugged. "It's what I do."

"Well, that's unhelpful."

"Why, you planning to run again?"

His eyes had a seriousness that made her stomach flip-flop. Or maybe it was just the baby moving. She spread a hand over her stomach and returned her gaze to the snow flitting against the windshield. "Of course I am. You have to know that."

"And you have to know I'd just find you again."

She ground her teeth, fighting the film of tears filling her vision.

"Boy or girl?" he asked.

It took Melody a moment to realize he was asking about the baby. She shrugged. "No idea."

"You don't want to know?"

"Sure I do. But doctors keep records."

Ash nodded. "Smart thinking. No wonder you were able to stay off the radar so long."

The praise warmed her, and even though he was technically the enemy, she found herself wanting to tell him more. It had been a long time since she'd held a real conversation with anyone other than herself and her unborn child. But her desire for discourse was cut short as he turned off the highway and downshifted to make a bumpy turn onto a snow-rutted road.

"Ugh, I have to pee again."

"There'll be a bathroom in a few minutes."

She clamped her legs together and examined the houses they were passing on either side of the road. Soon, the headlights bounced off a row of large metal hangars to the left and he pulled to a stop near a rent-a-can. "You can go there."

She wrinkled her nose. "How far are we from the airport?"

"This is it." He pointed beyond the hangars to where a cluster of small aircraft dotted the snowy pavement.

"Oh." The baby rolled again, and she decided it would be better to just get it over with instead of arguing. After freezing her ass off on a frigid toilet seat, she climbed back into the truck, glad for the blowing heater as she dug in her purse for hand sanitizer.

"Hang tight." Leaving the truck running, he opened his door and got out, heading for the outhouse.

Melody glanced over at the steering wheel. She could easily slide across the bench and drive away before he caught up. Her suitcase was in the back, her jewelry in her purse. She'd never driven a manual transmission, but how hard could it be? Her hand hovered over her seatbelt, every muscle coiled with anticipation.

Then she curled her fingers into a fist and dropped it back onto her lap. Even if she managed to make a getaway without stalling, he'd just track her down again. *And if not him, someone else.*

Sighing, she slumped back against the seat and forced herself to look away from the steering wheel. Much as she hated to admit it, she was tired of running. Tired of living in fear, of always looking over her shoulder. Would it be so bad to go back to Brennan? Marry him and inherit the money? Be a good little bitch and bear his children?

Her breath caught on a sob.

The door opened and Ash climbed back inside, giving her what might be described as a satisfied look.

And then she knew. "That was a test, wasn't it?" She scowled at him, regretting her hesitation to flee. "Asshole."

He didn't rise to her insult, driving a few hundred feet before coming to a stop next to a tiny blue and white plane. "Time to go."

Eyeing the aircraft doubtfully, she got out of the truck. "That's our plane?" It looked like something out of a cartoon, with only two doors and a tiny little propeller. "I'm pretty certain there's no bathroom in there, and this pregnant lady can't go more than an hour without using the facilities."

He chuckled and shoved her suitcase into the plane behind the two seats. "We'll be on the ground again in about forty minutes. Come on."

She climbed into the plane and fastened her harness. It was going to take them forever to reach Idaho in forty-minute increments. Not that she was complaining. The more often they stopped, the more chances she'd have to escape.

He fired up the aircraft. The roar of the engine was deafening, and she gladly placed the earmuff-thingies he gave her over her knitted hat, muffling the sound. As he taxied them toward the runway, she asked, "How long is it going to take us to get to Idaho?"

His voice crackled from the earmuffs, but she was fairly certain he said, "We're not going to Idaho."

The ground dropped out from beneath them, leaving her light-headed—but not with vertigo—with terror. Because if he wasn't taking her back to Brennan, then where the hell were they going?

CHAPTER FIVE

Until now, Ash had assumed Melody was denying their bond because of her entanglement with her pack Alpha, but the way she cowered against the Cessna's passenger door made him fear she was going to open it and jump to her death. *She truly doesn't sense our bond.*

The urge to use his Alpha voice—to compel her to trust him—was strong, but he resisted. He couldn't risk frightening her into doing anything stupid, especially while they were three thousand feet in the air.

Gripping the yoke with both hands, he kept his voice calm but firm. "We're going to my cabin until we can sort things out. You don't need to be afraid."

"There's no—sort out." Her voice cut in and out of the mic as she shook her head. "Ransom—more money—Brennan tears your head off."

"Brennan's not going to tear my head off." Ash wasn't worried; prison had taught him to hold his own against guys like Brennan. "You keep using this guy's name as a shield, yet I'm pretty sure he's the one you're trying to escape from."

"I'm not hiding behind anyone," she spat. "Fight him if you want. I'm just warning you that the guy has no morals."

His gaze shifted to her hands clasped over her stomach, and rage swelled in his chest as a story fell into place in his mind. "Did he rape you?"

Her entire body stiffened, and she exhaled shakily before responding. "Not that it's any of your business, but no." She swallowed and looked down at her lap. "Grandad said he was my mate. I thought… I was told it was my job to satisfy him."

Ash pressed his tongue to the back of his teeth and gripped the yoke hard enough to make his knuckles ache. He was going to track down this Brennan guy and rip his balls off. Then he was going to shove them down her grandfather's throat. "No one except your wolf can tell you who you're destined to mate."

She laughed, her voice on the verge of hysteria. "I don't have a wolf."

Ash sat up straighter. "Don't have a…" He sucked in a breath of her velvety, feminine scent, sifting through it, searching for what should be there—but wasn't. She was right; there was no wolf. He stared at her, all the preceding events taking on a new light. "You're still human?"

She crossed her arms. "Some bounty hunter you are. Don't even know what you're tracking."

Returning his gaze to the windshield, Ash thought over everything he'd just learned. She'd been born to a pack, so he'd assumed she'd gotten her spirit animal during puberty as most shifters did. He'd also assumed he hadn't detected her wolf because pregnancy was repressing the animal—also common among most shifters. "Now your rejection makes sense."

"What are you talking about?" Her face looked pale in the dim light from the dashboard.

Now that he knew why she hadn't acknowledged him, he could simply tell her. "We're mates."

"We're what?" She gaped at him.

"I'm your fated mate, Melody."

"The hell we are." She scowled. "You're delusional. Fated mates aren't real."

"Of course they're real. They're rare, but they exist." Putting the plane on autopilot, he leaned toward her, tilting his head to expose his throat. "Smell me. Maybe now that I've told you, your wolf will sense it."

She wrinkled her nose and leaned away. "Get bent."

Ash sighed, trying not to let this new unexpected development frustrate him. There had to be a way to convince her. "I'm sure your pack uses smell as much as mine does. Just give it a try."

Huffing, she continued to glower, then rolled her eyes and gave in. She stretched her neck toward him and sniffed delicately. "Nope." She shrugged and settled back against her seat. "Just your aftershave. I told you, I don't have a wolf."

"She's there. You just haven't met her yet."

"Even if I get an animal, she'll be weak. Defective."

He pulled back. "Why do you think that?"

"Mom's wolf is an omega."

No wonder Melody seemed to have issues. He knew some packs treated omegas as punching bags, or worse —slaves. His pack hadn't had an omega since he'd been a child, but he remembered his parents treating the meek old shifter with kindness.

"Omegas aren't defective," he said. "And I doubt you'll be one, anyway. You're too sassy." He winked at her, trying to lighten her mood.

She only frowned again and turned to look out her window. After a few minutes of silence, she said, "Grandfather's line has sired our pack's Alphas for generations, and my dad was the last in line. Grandfather kept hoping he'd take another wife, sire a worthy heir. But dad refused, even though Grandfather insisted there's no way she could produce an Alpha." She stopped talking for a minute, staring in silence at the snow-capped mountains below. When she spoke again, there was a hitch in her voice. "Dad died when I was eleven. I didn't have my wolf yet, and by the time I turned seventeen and still didn't have an animal, Grandfather said I was defective and passed leadership to Brennan."

Ash raised his eyebrows. "He couldn't wait? Some shifters don't find their animals until well into their twenties."

She shrugged. "Grandfather had a stroke, and a couple of pack members attempted to overthrow him. All the pack assets are in Grandfather's name, and I'm his only heir. So rather than face the potential usurpers one-by-one, he set up a dowry—a trust fund I won't inherit until I marry the pack Alpha—and announced a competition to become his successor, winner take all."

"Including his granddaughter." Ash had heard of these arranged marriages. And they made him want to vomit. "So if this happened when you were seventeen, why aren't you married yet?"

"I have until I turn thirty—two years. Then I have to marry him. That was one thing Mom did stand up to Grandfather about—giving my animal a chance to claim the position." She hugged herself, shoulders hunched. "Brennan punished her. He broke her arm."

Chalk one up for Mom. He whistled softly. "That took guts. Omegas don't stand up to anyone, let alone an Alpha."

"Well, if I ever get a wolf, it's bound to be an omega, so even if we are mates, you don't want me." She scoffed. "You might as well turn me in and get the bounty, because my pack will eventually hunt me down. One way or another, I'll end up tied to Brennan."

Talk of the bounty made his worries about his debt resurface, but he couldn't allow those thoughts to interfere with this moment with Melody. He could see her fighting tears, and longed to reach out to her, to reassure her he'd keep her safe. Instead, he gripped the yoke. After the way he'd bungled the kiss, he knew better than to touch her that way without asking. "We'll visit the glacier after the baby is born. I bet you'll connect with your wolf there. Sometimes the shifter gene needs a nudge to become active."

She turned to stare at him with wide eyes. "You mean the Source? I thought that was as much a myth as fated mates."

"It's real." They hit a patch of turbulence, and he adjusted their altitude. "I haven't been there, but I've talked to people who've experienced the magic first hand."

She turned to the front and leaned forward hopefully. "Can we go now?"

He shook his head. "No. It's dangerous if a mother drinks from the Source while pregnant. It could harm both you and your baby."

"Oh."

He pointed out the window toward a pale green ribbon flickering across the starlit sky. "But look. A promise from the spirits. You will get your animal."

She followed the play of light, eyes reflecting the glow. "What if my animal is weak? Or if it turns out I don't have one after all?"

"You could end up with a blind mole rat and it wouldn't matter to me. But my wolf insists you're going to get a wolf, and he's never wrong."

A hesitant smile flickered across Melody's lips, the first he'd seen. The sight of it warmed his soul. She licked her lips, relaxing against the seat. "Tell me about this cabin you're taking me to."

"It's my family's." Ash hadn't been back since getting out of prison, and had to admit he was both excited and nervous to see it again. He checked his GPS. They were almost to the edge of the lake that bordered his pack's territory. "It's a little rustic, but well off the beaten path. No one will look for you there."

Melody sighed. "You underestimate Brennan. He'll find me, eventually. And my family is going to come after the baby, no matter where I hide. Grandfather wants his legacy to carry on."

"Well, they can't have you or our baby. I'll protect you both."

She narrowed her eyes at him. "This baby isn't even yours. Why do you care who has it?"

"The child can't help who sired it. But if you'll let me, I'd like to be its father." He ignored the small doubt prodding the back of his mind. He'd been living out of the back of his truck and at cheap hotels once in a while to shower, but that wouldn't do for his mate and child. And now that he wasn't going to turn her in, he wouldn't get the bounty he'd been counting on. His pack could lose everything—including the cabin he was taking her to now.

"I'll… think about it," Melody said.

He hoped that was a whisper of trust in her tone. And he hoped he deserved it.

CHAPTER SIX

Melody clutched the handhold above the window as Ash banked the plane toward a pale, frozen lake. Within a few minutes, they bumped along the icy surface and slid to a stop a few feet from a rickety, snow-covered dock. The dark pointed tips of spruce trees formed a palisade along the shore, back-lit by the faint green glow of the aurora.

"Wait here. I'll bring the sled for you." Ash unbuckled and climbed out of the plane, shutting the door quickly to keep the heat in. He moved around the still propeller, stripping out of his shirt as he walked.

She'd seen pack members undress for a shift plenty of times, but never a man as gorgeous or as ripped as Ash. Moonlight painted his bare chest in silver light, gliding down the broad planes of his muscular back. The dark tattoos covering his arms and running over his chest and shoulder blades seemed to move with a life of their own. Then he shimmied out of his pants, and she sucked in a breath as the curves of his well-toned ass were laid before her like a visual feast.

Draping his discarded clothing over the plane's propeller, he met her gaze through the windshield and gave her a knowing grin. She snapped her mouth closed, hoping he hadn't noticed her practically drooling, and heat flooded her face as she looked away. She hadn't allowed herself to appreciate a beautiful man in years, not even on television. Brennan got angry if she so much as glanced at anyone but him.

Then what Ash had told her clicked into place. *Brennan's not my mate.* Ash, however, was—or so he claimed. If that was true, she was allowed to look.

She lifted her gaze and found Ash engulfed in a shower of silver sparks. Gray fur blossomed over his shoulders, forming a thick ruff along his neck and down his chest. His face lengthened into a muzzle with glowing yellow eyes, and he dropped to all fours, tail held straight back. He lifted his shaggy head and howled.

The sound of his wolf's voice sent a shiver into her bones, a jolt of pleasure she hadn't expected. She let out a slow breath, warmed by the sensation. Maybe he wasn't lying about the mate bond.

The gray wolf fixed his gaze on her, tongue lolling in a wolf smile, before turning to lope up the bank of snow and disappear among the dark trees.

She sat breathless for long moments, engulfed in the night's silence, mittened hands clamped between her knees. All the adrenalin and fear of the last few hours had drained out of her, and she watched the thin green mist of the aurora ripple across the sky. *No one except your wolf can tell you who you're destined to mate.* Ash's words skated through her. She usually felt numb when she contemplated her spirit animal, but now she felt… prickly. Like a static charge inside her was just waiting to be released.

Could Ash be right about everything?

She hardly knew him, yet their conversation in the plane made her want to trust him. She'd grown up believing true mates were a fairy tale. Believing her wolf, if it ever came, would be a liability to the pack. And Ash was offering all the dreams that she'd given up on after Dad died. A wolf, a mate, a family. He even seemed genuine about wanting to care for her child.

The compassionate way Ash talked to her gave her a feeling she hadn't experienced in a very long time —hope.

"I know nothing about him," she said out loud, words rising in frosty white puffs. She couldn't believe she was sitting in the middle of nowhere, contemplating spending the rest of her life with a perfect stranger.

She tried to picture the rough, tattooed bounty hunter cradling a baby and couldn't. Touching her in naughty places? Yes. Changing dirty diapers? Not so much. If she stayed with him, would he want more children of his own? Both fear and desire warred within her at that thought.

The cold pressed in around her, making her antsy. How much time had passed since Ash disappeared? She pulled out her phone. She hadn't checked the time since leaving her condo, but she guessed he'd been gone close to an hour.

She sat back against the seat, looking at the frosted-over windows with scenarios of being discovered frozen to death playing through her mind. People disappeared in Alaska all the time, and if anything happened to Ash, she'd be up shit creek. She checked her phone again; no reception.

Gulping, she clutched her phone against her chest. She could get out and try to find an area with reception, but she wasn't quite that desperate yet. Heart thundering in her ears, she searched the dash for a radio she could call out on. The switches and buttons made no sense to her, and she was afraid to touch anything.

Something lit up the frost obscuring the windshield, followed by the growing roar of a snowmobile. She wiped at the glass with a mitten, blowing on it to clear a spot, and caught a glimpse of a moving pinprick of light. In a few moments, a machine emerged from the trees, catching air as it sailed over a berm onto the ice. It skidded to a halt next to the plane.

The door swung open, and Ash grinned up at her. Relief flooded her, and she had the urge to throw herself gratefully into his arms. She wasn't going to die out here alone on the ice.

He'd donned an orange parka and jeans, a black ski hat pulled low over his forehead. "Sorry I took so long. I had to shovel a path to the door. Ready?"

Maybe she was deluding herself or it was the mate bond beginning to take hold, but she smiled and took his hand to get out of the plane.

He led her to the snowmobile. "Sorry I don't have a two-seater. You'll have to sit between my legs. I'll make a second trip to get your bag."

She'd never been on a machine like this before, and awkwardly straddled the seat before he got on behind her. He wedged himself tightly against her back, both arms coming around her to grip the handles. That same tingly feeling she'd experienced when he howled raced through her again, tingling up her arms and legs to center in her core.

She gripped the gas cap in front of her as they lurched forward. It felt like she'd left her stomach behind. Thankful for the solid wall of muscle behind her, she squinted against the cold air and watched the trees zip past as they followed his trail back through the trees.

The ride took about fifteen minutes, and she might've missed the cabin completely if she'd been alone. It was buried nearly to the eaves with snow, with at least another four feet piled on the roof. Slivers of warm yellow light peeked above the snow piles reaching nearly to the tops of the windows, and a path of freshly shoveled snow led down beneath a large portico. Ash drove down and pulled to a stop at the front entry where a porch light illuminated the walls of snow surrounding them, making her feel as if they'd entered a cave. A heavy wooden door had been carved with a charming scene of two wolves standing on a hill.

Leaving the engine idling, Ash helped her off the snowmobile and escorted her to the door, ushering her inside a small mudroom. "Go get warmed up. I'll be right back with your suitcase."

She turned to thank him, but was met by the heavy thud of the door. Outside, the sound of the snowmobile raced away. Alone again, she pulled off her mittens and stuffed them into her pockets. Her fingers were stiff with cold, her insides trembly, and she hoped this cabin wasn't too rustic to provide a hot shower.

The inner door to the house was closed, and the enclosed space smelled like campfire smoke and wet fur. Her stomach churned, reminding her she'd never eaten her sesame chicken. God, she really hoped there was food here she could eat.

Ignoring the coat pegs on the varnished log wall, she opened the inner door. A wall of smoke rolled over her, setting her coughing. She backed up, eyes stinging as she tried to see inside. The choking yellow haze was too thick.

She retreated to the outer door, smoke continuing to fill the mudroom. Was the cabin on fire? What should she do?

All she knew was she couldn't stay here.

Hurrying back out into the frigid air, she climbed the snowy path out of the portico and moved across the snow to put some distance between herself and the building. She'd heard of places like this exploding when flames reached propane tanks or other fuel.

Her right foot sank sharply through the crust, and she fell forward, bare hands stinging against the crystalized snow. Floundering back to her feet, still up to her hips in snow, she scrambled to put her mittens back on. She shivered at the sensation of ice melting under the hem of her coat and over the tops of her boots.

She cupped her hands around her mouth and screamed at the top of her lungs, "Ash!"

The distant buzz of a snowmobile gave her little hope that he'd heard her. Glancing up at the star-studded sky, she wrapped her arms around herself. Last time he'd been gone an hour. She prayed Ash would return before she froze to death.

CHAPTER SEVEN

Ash secured Melody's suitcase onto the back of the snowmobile, then grabbed the compact shovel and turned to dig out the grommets on the dock. He had to batten down the plane to prevent the wind from carrying it across the ice. As he dug, he thought gratefully of his sister, who had apparently ensured the generator had plenty of fuel to keep everything from freezing over. The additional heat from the wood stove should have the place toasty warm for Melody by now.

He couldn't help but imagine her sprawled naked on the bearskin rug, her lush curves beneath his hands. When she'd nestled her back against him on the snowmobile, his wolf had turned crazy with lust. He'd been battling a hard-on for what felt like hours and had to continue to remind himself that she didn't feel the same way he did, not yet. A small part of him worried she might never come around; it sounded as if her sexual experience with Brennan had been less than pleasant. She was bound to be hesitant—skittish, even. He had to be gentle. Take it slow. And even if she never accepted him, he was resolved to protect her and keep her safe.

Cinching the final tie-down on the plane, he headed toward the cabin, reveling in the fresh air on his face and the clear night sky overhead. He'd been away too long, and coming back to pack lands felt good, but also made his worry about foreclosure more intense. Melody's bounty would've taken care of the debt in one fell swoop; now he'd have to pick up several smaller jobs and settle for making the usual monthly payment.

As he neared the hazy glow of the cabin, he spotted a figure waving both arms frantically overhead. His heartbeat picked up. "Melody?"

Then he noticed the open mudroom door and the smoke rolling out from under the portico. He gunned the throttle, cutting through the powdery snow to reach her.

A fire out here spelled disaster. There was no fire service—hell, in the middle of winter there wasn't even a functional hose. The cabin would be reduced to ashes in a matter of hours. Blood racing, he pulled to a stop beside where Melody stood up to her hips in snow and lips almost blue, the churned trail behind her evidence of her struggle to escape.

"Are you all right?" He reached down to help her climb onto the machine in front of him. "What happened?"

"I opened the door to go inside, and smoke started pouring out." Her voice sounded scratchy and a little shaken. "I haven't seen any flames, but I didn't want to risk going inside."

His attention shot to the snow-laden roof, and he realized what had happened. "Shit. The stove pipe must be blocked." Normally, heat from the stove kept the pipe open, but no one had lived here all winter. He wrapped his arms around Melody and pulled her back against his chest. "You did good to get out. Hang tight. I need to unblock the chimney."

Drawing the snowmobile up to the side of the house, he stood on the seat behind Melody to reach the edge of the roof. He pulled himself up and slogged through the snow toward the pipe. The gray snow around the vent had already begun to melt from the rising heat, allowing a thin trickle of smoke to escape, and he quickly cleared the cap with both hands.

Smoke gushed toward the stars, and he backed away, eyes stinging. The air inside the cabin would take hours, if not days, to be breathable again. He lowered himself back to the snowmobile, apologizing to Melody for the cascade of powder that came with him.

"Can we go inside now?" she asked through chattering teeth.

"It'll be too smoky for a while. My sister's place is about a mile from here. We'll crash there tonight." Carmen was likely mad at him for not coming back right away after getting out of prison, and he might end up sleeping outside as his wolf for the night, but he didn't think she'd deny Melody a bed.

Melody couldn't stop shivering, even when Ash climbed onto the snowmobile behind her and molded his muscular thighs against her hips. The chill was so bone deep, it was hard to breathe, and the pressing darkness made her want to curl up in the snow and sleep.

"How long were you standing out here?" he asked over the buzz of the engine, pulling away from the cabin.

"S-since you left." She hunched her shoulders, leaning back against his chest. Even with his arms around her to grip the handlebars, she couldn't stop shivering.

"Shit." He revved the engine and took them careening between the trees.

She was glad he had her caged between his arms and legs, because she wasn't certain she could've held on for the bumpy ride. After what felt like forever, they pulled to a stop next to another cabin.

Ash cut the engine and dismounted. But Melody's muscles refused to move until he pulled her upright.

The cabin's front door opened, and a child's voice called, "Hello?"

A tiny girl with two dark braids and gray eyes peered out at them. Ash asked, "Roxie?"

"Mom!" shouted the girl, slamming the door.

Melody glanced at Ash, suddenly worried they'd have to get back on the machine. "Are they going to let us in?"

"Don't worry." Ash let them in without knocking, then guided her to sit on the boot bench.

Despite the warmth seeping through the bench onto the backs of her legs, the cold was stuck like daggers in her skin. She couldn't even get a grip on her mittens to remove them as Ash bent to remove her boots.

"I c-can't feel my toes," she said. "Do you think I have frostbite?"

"I don't think so, but you're hypothermic for sure." He helped her fumble out of her mittens. "I'll have you warmed up soon."

A woman's voice came from behind him. "Ash? Oh my God, Ash!"

Someone flung themselves against his back, arms clasping his waist and nearly knocking him over into Melody's lap as he helped unzip her parka.

He patted the woman's forearm without turning around. "Fire up your sauna. I need to get her warm."

A grown-up version of the little girl at the door leaned around him. "Who is she? What happened?"

Melody tried to smile at her, but Ash shooed the woman away. "It's a really long story. I'll explain later. Just go."

"Fine." The woman disappeared as Ash finished removing Melody's outer wear.

Standing on wobbly legs, Melody couldn't even manage to take one step before she collapsed back to the bench. She'd never realized how cold could sap someone's strength. Her hand went to her belly. "Do you think the baby is okay?"

"I'm sure it's fine. That's the warmest place it could be right now." Ash picked her up and carried her into the house.

Inside, two older children sat on the floor in front of a coffee table strewn with crayons and paper while the small girl from the doorway stood behind them near the sofa, watching with wary eyes.

The boy asked, "Uncle Ash? You're back!"

"Hi, Rory." Ash nodded as he strode past. "I'll talk to you in a bit, okay?"

In the wood-lined sauna, he pushed aside a couple of toy cars and laid Melody on the bench. He smelled so good and felt so warm. She had to force herself to let go of his neck.

The woman—she assumed it must be his sister—came in behind him with an armful of split wood. "Sorry about the mess. The kids warmed up in here after sledding."

The wood bench felt hot against her frigid hands. "Ow! The bench is so hot."

"No, it's not." Ash grabbed a towel from a nearby shelf and tucked it beneath her. "You're just extra sensitive because you got too cold. We'll get you warm soon."

He removed her socks, and she stared woozily at her feet. In the light from the single overhead bulb, her skin looked ashen and the toenails a bit blue, but she could wiggle her toes. She let out a breath of relief.

The woman placed the wood inside the potbelly stove, glowing flames rising to life almost immediately. "Watch the temperature."

"I know," he growled, cradling one of Melody's feet between his palms. The warmth of his touch felt amazing.

"Don't bite my head off." Shooting him a reproachful glance, she clanged the stove door shut and moved to the exit. "I just wanted to make sure you knew saunas and pregnancy don't mix. I'll go heat water for tea."

Ash waited until she closed the door, then shucked out of his parka. Melody's eyes widened. He was bare-chested, and this close, his muscles seemed even more ripped. His tattoos flowed like black flames over his shoulders and chest, and with what seemed to be a will of their own, her fingers rose to trace a curl.

He froze. "If you touch me like that, I can't be responsible for what happens."

She managed to drag her gaze upward and found his eyes, two dark pools of desire.

Fingers still glued to his skin, she gulped. What was wrong with her? Was it the heat? This man had all but kidnapped her, and now she was ogling his body. Yet she couldn't deny the pressure building in her center, a craving she'd never experienced. It had been months since she'd experienced so much as a handshake with another person, and Ash could probably make her feel things she'd never imagined. *He claims to be my fated mate. Is it so wrong to want him?*

After all, she was a free woman. Free to choose who to be with, at least until Brennan eventually caught her. This moment, this piece of time, could be hers and hers alone. The thought of Ash's hands on her drove her already pounding heart into a frenzy.

Licking her lips, she locked her gaze with his. "I want you."

The hunger in his eyes burned hotter, the golden glow of his wolf's presence sparking like matches. But he shook his head. "You're not thinking straight because of the cold."

She took his hands and put them on her hips, guiding them beneath the hem of her shirt. His palms heated the bare skin of her waist. "I've heard the only cure for hypothermia is skin-to-skin contact."

He groaned as she lifted her arms, inviting him to slide the shirt over her head. His hesitation lasted less than a heartbeat before he pulled the garment up and off, eyes glued to her breasts straining against a lacy white bra. She'd grown fuller since the pregnancy, but hadn't had money to invest in new underthings yet.

"God, you're sexy." His voice was so low, it was almost a growl.

He leaned forward and brushed his lips across her skin just above the cupped lace. His breath was hot against her cold skin, and she sucked in a breath, nipples tightening as he reached behind her to unclasp her bra. He slid the straps from her shoulders, bending down to suck a nipple.

She shuddered as he licked and sucked her into fiery tingles of pleasure. Her hands explored the delicious planes and angles of his shoulders and arms. His skin was nearly hairless, yet coarser than her own, and she let her fingers creep to the back of his neck.

He toyed with her breasts until she was panting, then pushed her back against the bench. His hands fumbled for her fly, releasing the button and zipper as he ran his tongue down the gentle swell of her belly to the edge of her matching lace panties.

"You smell so fucking good." He growled, a sound that made every muscle in her body tingle.

She lifted her hips to help him pull off her jeans. She couldn't believe she was doing this. Pregnant, on the run, and about to give herself to a man who'd abducted her to the middle of nowhere, no less. But he was so damn hot. She didn't want to stop.

He tossed the pants aside and dipped down to drag his teeth over her panties, nipping lightly.

Jolts of desire surged through her pelvis, and heat flooded her center. "Oh, God."

Panting, she closed her eyes and let her head fall back. She'd never imagined wanting anything as badly as she wanted his touch right now. To feel him explore every inch of her body.

He rolled her panties down her hips, palms searing trails of heat down the outside of her thighs. Then he began massaging up one calf and thigh. As the hand between her legs neared her center, she arched her back, core tight with anticipation.

"That feels so good," she whispered.

But disappointment warred with pleasure as his touch bypassed her pussy and continued massaging her hips and gently over her belly until he reached her breasts. One knee slid between her legs, prodding her thighs apart while his big palms worked heated magic over her skin. She opened her eyes to find him licking his lips.

"Kiss me," she demanded.

He complied, bending to meet her mouth. His tongue swept across her lips, opening them like a flower before he delved between her teeth, meeting her in a passionate dance that left her breathless.

Her hands circled his chest to pull his naked torso down against her, covering her with his heat and weight. She rolled her hips so her clit rubbed against his thigh.

He nipped her lower lip, leaning into her with exactly the right amount of pressure. "See how good we could be together?"

She nodded, breathless, knowing she was thinking with her vagina instead of her head. But her body was on fire, and there was only one way to quench it.

Nuzzling along her jaw, he kissed her behind her ear and gently sucked her neck, the rasp of his stubble exciting her as he trailed down to her shoulder.

Something inside her shifted, the image of Brennan flooding her mind as Ash's mouth approached the claiming mark the Alpha had given her at the curve of her neck and shoulder. Brennan had said the bite made her off-limits to other shifters.

Ash paused at the scar, a low growl rolling through him.

She tensed. "Brennan—"

"Don't say his name," Ash cut her off, gently nipping the mark.

For a brief moment, she thought he might place his claim over the Alpha's. Instead, he continued kissing down her shoulder, across her chest, nuzzling each breast in turn.

She panted, torn between confusion and pleasure as his hands brushed down her sides, worshiping her, soothing her. This time, he didn't bypass her pussy. He paused at her apex, breath fanning her lower lips before his tongue snaked out to part her folds. Her hands circled the back of his head, urging him deeper.

She needed him. Needed to feel him inside her, needed him to push away all memories of past invasions of her body. "Make me yours."

He circled her clit in a languid move that had her entire body vibrating with pleasure. Slowly, surely, he built up a rhythm, sucking and stroking. She bucked against him, release almost within reach. He flicked her with his hot, slippery tongue and dipped his fingers between her legs, one shallow plunge that made her gasp.

Wetness coated her thighs, and his finger teased her opening before sliding inside with agonizing slowness. He stroked her inner ridges, tongue circling her clit. He increased his pressure and rhythm until the tension inside her thrummed like a well-played instrument. When he added a second finger, she came undone. Her own cry filled her ears as her insides pulsed in wave after wave of ecstasy.

Only after she'd relaxed in satiated bliss did he withdraw his fingers. She opened her eyes to find him licking them clean, eyes aglow with the presence of his wolf. He still wore his jeans, but the lump at his crotch was a clear indication of his unabated arousal.

She looked up at him, still hazy from passion. "Why aren't you naked?"

He grinned and shook his head, laying down on the bench and spooning her against his chest. "Our first time is going to be special, not a frenzy of passion in my sister's sauna."

Reality crashed back around her, and she stared at the closed sauna door. In the background, the theme song for Sponge Bob played loudly, probably to cover up her moaning. "Oh, God. Your sister. Her kids—"

"Don't worry about them."

"Don't tell me not to worry." She sat up and pulled free of him, looking around for her clothes. She winced at the sight of several toys shoved beneath the corner of the bench they were on. Kids used this sauna, too. What must Ash's sister think? She closed her eyes, feeling embarrassment overtake the flush of passion. "What will she think of me?"

"She'll understand. Are you warm yet?"

"I think you know the answer." Melody located her bra in the far corner and picked it up, disliking the thought of donning the constricting band.

She turned to find Ash sitting up and watching her with hungry eyes, holding out her lace panties. But her gaze went straight to his fly, swollen to the seams and about ready to burst. Just how big was he? God, how she wanted to find out.

He waved the panties. "I'll never calm down if you keep looking at me like that. Get dressed so we can go relieve my sister's curiosity."

Blushing at her own wanton thoughts, she snatched her panties from his hand and dressed, wondering how she was going to face the woman whose sauna she'd just debauched.

CHAPTER NINE

Ash pointed Melody to the bathroom and borrowed one of Carmen's boyfriend's tee shirts before heading to the front room. The television was blasting, and the kids were parked on the floor, eyes glued to the screen. His sister sat in a rocking chair, stabbing her needle into her latest embroidery project.

Spotting him, she gave him a stern look and headed to the kitchen. Obviously, she wanted him to follow her.

He gulped, steeling himself for the berating he knew was coming.

A pot of caribou spaghetti bubbled on the stovetop in the cozy kitchen, and his stomach growled. Carmen was an awesome cook, and the scent brought back memories of years past. How long had it been since he'd enjoyed a home-cooked meal? But before he could ask for some, his sister rounded on him, gray eyes flashing. "Couldn't you at least keep it in your pants until you were alone? I've got impressionable kids here."

He frowned. "Hey, it's not like you and Robin don't—"

"Leave that asshat's name out of this. He's been out of the picture for over a year—as if you'd know."

Shit. He really was behind on things. Then again, his sister was always taking on "fixer-uppers" so he shouldn't be surprised. "I didn't mean to—"

"What are you doing here, anyway? Go to Dad's. I kept it up for you."

"I noticed, thanks," he said. "But I didn't clear the chimney before starting a fire, so the place needs to air out for a bit first."

She let out a sigh of disgust. "I have to do fucking everything for you, don't I?"

Ash sighed and pressed his tongue to the back of his teeth, refusing to be baited. He couldn't blame her for resenting him. He'd inherited the Alpha power when it should've been her; he'd proven he was unfit several times.

Running a hand through his hair, he poured every ounce of sincerity into his voice he could muster. "I'm sorry, Carmen. I really am grateful for the upkeep, and I'll find a way to pay you back. Just be nice to Melody, okay? We'll be out of your hair tomorrow morning."

"What's up with that, anyway?" She hooked a thumb toward the sound of running water in the bathroom. "You've been out of prison less than a year and already knocked up some bitch?"

"Don't." The word emerged as a guttural growl just shy of an Alpha command.

Carmen bared her teeth, and he sensed her wolf rising to the surface, ready for a fight. His own wolf reared up, ready for a tussle, but then her attention shifted to the living room.

He turned to find Melody standing hesitantly at the kitchen threshold. He smiled encouragingly and held out an arm. "Hey. Come meet my sister. Carmen, this is…" he hesitated, unsure how Melody might react, but then decided fuck it. The truth was the truth. He moved over to stand by her side. "This is my mate, Melody."

Melody bit her lip but said nothing.

Carmen's dark brows shot up in surprise. "You've got to be kidding." She sized the two of them up, then her shoulders sagged. "Fuck. Of course you found your mate. You get everything."

Melody shook her head. "I don't want to cause any trouble. I didn't ask to come here."

Carmen shot Ash a baleful glance as she pulled out a wooden stool at the breakfast bar and gestured for Melody to take a seat. "Honey, none of this is your fault. Sit. Let me make you some tea."

Glancing at Ash, Melody edged forward but didn't sit. "Just to be clear, the baby isn't Ash's."

"You don't need to defend my brother to me." Carmen plopped a mug down on the counter in front of the stool and started heaping a plate with spaghetti. "I'm going to think he's an asshole no matter what."

Ash ignored the barb, nudging Melody toward the stool as Carmen put some garlic bread in the toaster oven.

His stomach rumbled. "You're in for a treat, Melody. Carmen's the best cook in the pack."

Melody shook her head, her face a little green. "I couldn't, really. Just tea, please."

"Nonsense," replied Carmen. "You're eating for two, and you've endured a traumatic experience—getting saddled with my brother." She chortled at her own joke, and even Ash had to smile at her jab. "You need comfort food."

The scent of buttery garlic bread filled the kitchen, and Ash squeezed Melody's shoulder. "Just try it. If you don't want it, I'll eat it."

"Back off, mister." Carmen put a hunk of toasted bread on the plate and set it in front of Melody.

Smiling politely, Melody picked up the bread and nibbled a corner. Her eyes lit up, and she took a bigger bite, chewing hungrily.

"See? Told you," Ash said, snagging another piece of bread from the toaster as Carmen started filling a second plate. *God bless her.* "Thanks, Carmen."

"Wow, this is amazing," Melody said around a mouthful of spaghetti. "I haven't been able to stomach anything but sesame chicken lately. Thank you."

"You're welcome." Carmen leaned back against the counter. "Mates, huh? How did you two find each other?"

Melody shrugged. "I caught him rifling through my underwear."

It took a moment for Ash to react, then heat flooded his neck and face as he spluttered for words.

Carmen burst out laughing and handed Ash a loaded plate. "Awesome. Sounds just like something he'd do."

Ash turned his attention to twirling a bite on his fork, glad for an excuse to look away. "I was looking for clues, okay?"

"He broke into my condo." Melody licked butter off her fingers.

"Ash!" Carmen gasped. "You're going to end up back in prison if you're not careful."

Melody paused, fork halfway to her mouth. "You were in prison?"

Ash's insides clenched. Melody needed to know about his past, but this wasn't exactly a comfortable moment to reveal his darkest secrets. Carmen would be all too happy to keep poking until he cried uncle.

His sister put her hands on her hips. "He didn't mention that yet, huh? My brother's a murderer."

Ash scowled at her. "Not murder, involuntary manslaughter. There's a big difference."

"Tell that to the dead girl."

The greenish tinge had returned to Melody's face, and she looked ready to bolt for the door. She gulped as if the spaghetti wanted to come back up. "You killed someone?"

Feeling cornered, Ash stepped backward until his hips hit the edge of the counter and crossed his arms. That terrible day would always be fresh on his mind. But regret could be paralyzing, and he tried not to think about it. *You have to tell Melody some time.*

Swallowing, he looked down at the scuffed linoleum. "I was hunting a guy who'd skipped bail. Cornered his ex-girlfriend in a hotel room and tried to use my Alpha voice to get her to reveal his location." He took a deep breath, recalling her terrified hazel eyes in the seconds before she turned toward the window. "Turns out she was more scared of him than she was of me. She jumped out a fourth-story window rather than give him up."

"Oh," Melody gasped.

He looked up to find her covering her mouth with both hands. The horror in her eyes mirrored his own, and he quickly finished the story, wanting this conversation to end. "I served eight years for involuntary manslaughter and had to pay her family ninety-thousand dollars."

"*We* had to pay her family," Carmen clarified. "The pack. We'd already mortgaged everything to send him to law school before this happened, then we had to mortgage it again to hire a lawyer and pay his debt."

He looked at his sister in silence, jaw clenched. There was no rebuttal. She was correct. Every bit of her anger was justified.

Carmen punched him in the arm, hard enough to make him flinch. "Worse, this asshole's been out of prison for months and hasn't bothered to come back to see us. Some Alpha."

"I'm not your Alpha," he snarled. "I don't know how many times I have to tell everyone that." He would never use his power again, not after what he'd done with it.

She let out a huff. "You don't get to choose if you're Alpha. The pack does. They want you."

"Why the hell do they insist it's me? You could lead them far better than I can."

"I *am* leading them, but I don't have the Alpha power like you do. They're at each other's throats, and when they *are* getting along, it's like a frat party gone off the rails. Yates is acting weird again, chasing people off his property. I haven't heard from the Sinclaire family since they went to fish camp six months ago. And some members of Old Man Quentin's pack are squatting in the old cabin at the creek bend. I can't get them to leave."

Ash's hackles rose at the mention of Quentin's pack. They'd been pushing his pack's western boundary for generations, and would snatch up the deed to the property if Ash couldn't keep up payments on the mortgage. *Would that be so bad?* He rubbed the back of his neck. "Maybe we should just sell him the territory. Let him annex everything, including the pack."

"How can you say that!" Carmen slugged him again, harder this time. "Mom and Dad are rolling over in their graves. We need you, Ash. Even if you are a dick."

"You know what happens when I try to be Alpha. I can barely keep my own life on the straight and narrow, let alone deal with other people."

"Well, too bad. You have a mate now and a child on the way. They need a pack, and so do you."

That realization made his blood turn to ice. He looked at Melody.

Her cheeks were flushed, eyes wide. What was she thinking? Hell, what had *he* been thinking? He couldn't take care of a mate, not like she deserved. He'd let his hormones get the better of him. Let his wolf's instincts make his choices.

But whether he formalized a mate bond or not, he didn't want to turn her over to that asshole Brennan, even if the bounty would solve his pack's money problems. So what was he supposed to do with her?

"I need some air." Pushing off the counter, he stalked toward the exit, shucking out of his pants along the way to the front door. A good long run with his wolf would help set his head straight.

CHAPTER TEN

Melody gaped at the empty space Ash had just been as the sound of the front door thudding closed shook the house. "Where's he going?"

"Who knows?" said Carmen from beside her. "He's an asshole."

Despite Melody's shock, a protective urge rose inside her, a little like the feeling she'd had when she discovered she was pregnant. She wasn't happy Ash had gone off and left her here, but she also didn't think he deserved his sister's ire. *Mates are supposed to stand up for each other, right?*

She turned to Carmen with a frown. "Don't call him that. He has some valid concerns about being an Alpha."

Carmen scowled and shook her head. "The pack is disintegrating without him. He needs to step up and get over it."

"I understand you're angry, but Ash is obviously feeling a lot of guilt about that girl." She swallowed, nervous about saying more. "Maybe goading and punching him makes him feel worse."

Carmen flushed, looking at her hands. "Shit, you sound like my mom." She sighed and retrieved a mug from the cupboard, pouring herself some tea. "I'm just so angry at him for abandoning us."

Glad Carmen hadn't taken her words the wrong way, Melody nodded in agreement.

"Let's talk about something else." Carmen sat on the stool beside Melody's. "Tell me why Ash was in your apartment."

Melody picked up her fork and toyed with the noodles on her plate. She'd spent so many weeks alone, hiding her secrets, worrying about a wrong word getting back to her pack, that talking felt strange. But Carmen listened intently, and before Melody knew it, the story was spilling out.

When she reached the part about the inheritance, her voice cracked. "All Grandfather cares about is keeping the Alpha line in our family, so he's forcing me to marry Brennan." Melody gritted her teeth, holding back the shudder that wanted to rip through her. "At least not having a wolf kept me from being forced down the aisle already."

Carmen nodded thoughtfully. "Shit, I think my spirit animal would've stayed in hiding, too, if showing up meant I had to marry someone like your pack Alpha."

Melody felt like vomiting. Could Carmen be right, and her wolf was that weak? Then again, she couldn't blame her wolf for hiding as she remembered Brennan's touch. His smell. His derisive leer as he instructed her to strip. "Whatever happens, he can't learn about the baby."

"I get it. I have three rugrats of my own who I'd prefer had nothing to do with their fathers, and I sort of liked those assholes at the beginning. You didn't even get that pleasure." Carmen rose and refilled their mugs. "At least no one can keep you from your mate now that you've found him."

Melody wrapped her fingers around the hot mug, holding on longer than was comfortable. "You really believe Ash is my fated mate? He wouldn't lie to me?"

A stunned look washed over Carmen's features. "What do you mean? You don't know?"

"I don't have a wolf, remember?" Melody's chest heaved as she tried to hold back tears. She did not know if they were tears of fear or relief at the moment. It had been a long day, and a longer time being scared and on the run. The thought of finally being safe, of not looking over her shoulder anymore, was overwhelming.

Carmen retrieved a box of tissues from the corner. "Go ahead and let it out, honey. It's going to be all right, I promise." She patted Melody gently between the shoulder blades. "I talk smack about Ash because he's my brother, but he's actually a really stand-up guy. If he says you're his mate, you should believe him."

"I've been forced into things and lied to my entire life." Melody looked down at her plate, eyes burning. "It's hard to believe someone might actually tell me the truth."

Something tugged the edge of her blouse, and she looked down to find a mini version of Carmen looking up at her. The little girl couldn't be more than three, with two short dark braids and a smudge of what looked like purple marker on her chin. She lay her cheek against Melody's thigh and patted her hip. "Don't cwy. It'll be awight, honey."

Melody swiped her wet cheeks and put a hand on the girl's head. "Thank you, sweetie."

"Come on, Rebel. It's bedtime." Carmen hoisted the child onto her hip. "Let's find a nightgown for Aunt Melody." She winked at Melody as she carried the girl away.

Aunt Melody. What a strange notion. As an only child, she'd never really imagined having nieces and nephews. *If I marry Ash, Carmen will be my sister.*

She smiled to herself. She liked Carmen. Liked having another woman to talk to who was obviously just as strong as any of the men around her, even if she wasn't an Alpha. It was so different from talking to her mother, who equivocated everything. Even her friends in school had been untrustworthy, including her one minute and snubbing her the next.

The clock on the stove rolled over to seven as Melody finished her spaghetti, her stomach surprisingly content. If she ended up staying with Ash, she'd have to get Carmen to teach her how to make it.

Wondering how long Ash would stay out, she rinsed her dishes in the sink and returned to the front room. The coffee table had been pushed aside, and the sofa pulled out into a hide-a-bed. A neatly folded nightgown lay on top of the thick blankets, obviously waiting for her. Deeper in the house, she could hear Carmen tucking the kids in and their small voices chirping complaints about going to bed before Uncle Ash came home.

"I know how you feel, kid," Melody whispered as she moved to the window and peered outside at the snow and trees, picturing Ash's wolf running across the snow under the moonlight.

A familiar ache of longing filled her, a desire to meet her own spirit animal. Had her wolf really stayed dormant to keep her out of Brennan's clutches, as Carmen suggested? It was something Melody'd never considered. The possibility made sense when she thought about it. An omega would stay in hiding to avoid trouble.

Yet a part of her also wondered if her wolf had been waiting for Ash.

Are you in there, wolf? she thought to herself, as she had so many times in her adolescence and beyond. But as always, there was no response.

She pressed her fingertips against the cold windowpane, watching the glass turn foggy around her touch. The baby felt heavy in her belly tonight, though it couldn't be much bigger than her cell phone yet. In a few short months, she'd be a mother—and Ash had asked to take care of them both. Would that be so bad? Carmen said he was a good man, and he'd shown he could be tender. Caring. Responsible.

Except for when it comes to leading a pack. He was sexy and dominant, but he wasn't like Brennan. He wasn't cruel. He considered his Alpha power a duty rather than a right, which was the exact opposite of the man her family wanted her to marry.

Brennan had killed for his position—literally. The competition Grandfather had orchestrated to name his successor was supposed to have ended when the final contestant yielded. But Brennan's wolf had been ferocious, almost rabid in his attack. His opponent had died wrapped in the coils of his own entrails. No one else had stepped up to challenge after that.

She put a palm flat against her stomach. Brennan could not find out about the baby, let alone be allowed to raise it. She didn't even trust her mother with the task. For her family, her baby would be nothing more than a tool, a means to maintain control of a powerful pack and the money associated with it. The child had to be protected, and she couldn't do it by herself.

Whether or not she believed in fated mates, she needed to stay close to Ash.

CHAPTER ELEVEN

*A*sh veered toward a game trail along the creek near Carmen's house, claws digging into the packed snow. His head swam with all the decisions he had to make. He hadn't needed to plan ahead for anything since college, his years in prison demanding only his instinct to survive from day to day. Since getting out, all he'd cared about was making enough money to clear his debt. Being a lone wolf had suited him fine.

Except now he had Melody to consider, and whether she accepted him or not, she needed a pack. His pack. And his pack needed an Alpha. *It can't be me.* Yet Carmen insisted he was the only one who could hold them together.

Trouble was, he didn't trust his self-control, not when it came to his power.

He raced across the snow, panting as he leaped over a fallen tree. Weaker shifters and even many humans were easily compelled by an Alpha's command. It was one thing to call on his Alpha power to survive in prison—the men in there only understood force. But he'd already cost one innocent her life. What if he made another mistake?

We won't, his wolf insisted.

Ash slowed his gait. There was only one way he could be sure he never made the same mistake again, and his wolf wasn't going to like it. *If we stay here, I must lead as a human. I can't use our Alpha powers.*

His wolf chuffed, frosty breath rising into the night sky. *Impossible.*

Controlling his wolf's urges might prove more difficult than controlling the pack, Ash realized, leaping over a fallen tree. As he landed, a skunky, green odor hit him —not smoke, but living, growing marijuana. It was coming from the south, toward Yates's place. And it reeked more than one or two potted plants would warrant.

What's he up to? Ash veered right, coming to a stop at the edge of the tree line. Ahead, Yates' cabin was nothing but a shadow under the light of the setting moon. The pungent scent of weed choked the air. Marijuana was legal in Alaska, but you had to have permits to grow it commercially, and Ash doubted Yates had bothered. The man had been a few years ahead of Ash in school and had spent a year in juvie for dealing out of his locker.

The sound of a generator kicked on, thrumming through the cold, still air. Ash drew closer, noting a thin slice of pinkish light escaping along the edge of the aluminum foil covering a window. Carmen said Yates was keeping people away, and now he knew why.

Hot anger rose inside him. An illegal grow operation could not only cost the pack in fines, it could land multiple people in prison, himself included. Hackles up, he advanced onto the packed snow path leading to the front door before shifting to human form.

Most pack members kept spare clothing stashed near the door for modesty's sake, and he found a rolled-up pair of sweatpants and a tee shirt in the newspaper box. He shoved the shirt back into the box, opting for just the pants. They were vastly oversized, forcing him to hold them up with one hand to prevent them from slipping off his hips.

Bare feet sinking into the biting snow, he took a deep breath to steady himself. This was going to be a good test to see if he could handle things without using his Alpha power. Before he could knock, the door swung open, and he was confronted by the muzzle of a shotgun.

A dark pair of eyes glittered in the depths of a dim entryway. "Who the fuck's there?"

Ash's Alpha power swelled automatically, and it took every ounce of control to keep the Alpha compulsion out of his voice. "Put it down, Yates."

The other man lowered the weapon and inched forward into the moonlight, his square jaw covered in at least three days' worth of reddish stubble. A hank of brown hair flopped over one of the man's eyes, and he flipped his chin to toss it out of the way. "Ash? Hell, man, no one told me you were back! Come in before all the heat escapes."

Ash stepped inside, nearly choking on humidity and the thick, jungle-like scent of growing weed. Yates closed the door with a thump, then skirted Ash to fling open the interior door. Fuchsia-tinted light streamed into the room.

Bare feet sticking to the linoleum underfoot, Ash followed Yates inside. What had once been a living room was now a forest of toothy leaves. Every square foot of space held a potted plant, and the ceiling had been fitted with rows of LED lights. The low hum of several fans circulating air ran in the background.

Through a gap in the foliage, Ash could see the kitchen was also a jungle of plants. "What the fuck's going on here?"

Yates set the butt of his shotgun on the floor, one hand gripping the muzzle like a walking stick, and looked around proudly. "Gonna pay down the pack's mortgage."

Ash's stomach soured. Yates was worried about losing the property and trying to prevent it the best way he knew how. "I appreciate you wanting to help, but this," Ash gestured around the room, "is going to end in trouble. Get rid of it. I'll handle the debt."

"No can do." Yates cocked an eyebrow. "I always pay back what I owe."

"What do you mean?"

"Your dad bailed me out of jail twice, plus paid a bunch of money for legal fees. I promised to pay it all back, and just 'cause he's gone doesn't mean my debt's clear."

Ash froze. He'd never been great at tracking expenses, but had always assumed the pack debt was all because of him. "My dad posted bail for you?"

"Yeah. And before you start lecturing, hear me out. I have a friend with a grow license who says he'll take the product off my hands for a good price. It's not exactly on the up-and-up, but it's easy money if you know what you're doing, and I do. I should get about thirty grand for this new batch alone."

That gave Ash pause. He took a step back and looked at the nearby fuzzy, Christmas tree-shaped branches. He knew little about plants, especially weed, but the buds on these things were bowing the plants over with their weight. They had to be near ready for harvest. A *lot* of harvest.

He sighed, adjusting the sweats drooping around his hips. He wasn't the most law-abiding citizen himself, and had even taken a few questionable bounty jobs since getting out of prison; criminals tracking down other criminals tended to pay best. But he now had Melody's wellbeing to consider, and couldn't take care of her from a jail cell. "You know everyone within five hundred feet can smell this place, right? If someone turns you in, the entire pack could suffer."

Yates snorted. "Yeah, but who's gonna do that? The only ones out here are pack members."

"What about this friend who says he'll buy everything?"

"He's cool. He wanted to hire me but said my rap sheet would give him headaches with the marijuana board. This setup is win win, believe me."

Ash wanted to believe him. Thirty thousand would be enough to make payments for several months and give him time to take on a few good bounty jobs to pay the rest. "How soon?"

"I have my first batch drying already. I figure I can get it out at the end of this week."

A wash of relief filled Ash. He'd been unwilling to admit even to himself how worried he was about making this next payment, but the end of the week would be just in time to keep the bank from foreclosing. And it would give him time to make sure Melody was settled instead of abandoning her to take another job. *The benefit outweighs the risk.* Wasn't that the sort of decision a pack leader made?

"Fuck it." Ash turned toward the exit. "Just keep me updated, all right?"

"You bet."

Ash stepped out of the baggy sweats and opened the door, the cold air sending goosebumps over his skin.

"Hey, Ash?"

He looked over his shoulder.

"Glad to have you back."

Ash grunted and closed the door before letting his wolf once more take over. Overhead, the northern lights played green and pink splashes across the stars, bathing the snow in pastel light reminiscent of the grow lights in the cabin. Was it a sign? He didn't know.

He trotted away from the cabin, angling his way back toward the lake. At the bank, he paused, looking across the darkness at the line of trees. This was pack territory—*his* territory. And he'd do whatever it took to keep it. Raising his muzzle, he howled.

In the distance, an answering howl rolled across the snowy treetops, followed by a second. The voice of his pack. A sudden sense of belonging welled up inside him. As he loped back toward his sister's cabin, he hoped he wasn't deluding himself.

CHAPTER TWELVE

$\mathcal{M}$elody stretched and opened her eyes in the darkness, taking a moment to remember where she was. She hadn't intended to fall asleep when she'd lain atop the covers, but the bed had been more comfortable than she'd expected. Now she had to pee. She started to get up and realized she was covered with a blanket; someone had tucked her in.

"Morning," a low, familiar voice rumbled through the darkness.

Ash had come back.

She froze, eyes wide in the murky illumination from a nightlight in the hallway. Ash sat in the rocking chair facing her. He'd dressed, broad shoulders covered by a form-fitting tee and long legs clothed in jeans. His glittering gaze met hers, and her heart fluttered.

"What time is it?" she asked.

"Early. Or late, depending on your point of view."

She let a heartbeat pass, wondering if he might volunteer more. Like where he'd gone and why. But he didn't. So she asked, "Everything okay?"

He leaned forward and turned on the lamp, bringing the living room's log walls back into view. "Yeah, I think so. We should talk."

That sounded ominous. Had he changed his mind? Maybe he'd realized she wasn't his mate after all. Crap, what if he wanted to turn her in and collect the bounty? Her heartbeat kicked into overdrive. "About what?"

"Not now. Let's wait until we're in private." He lifted his chin toward the hallway behind her.

She looked over her shoulder in time to see a small face duck behind the edge of the wall.

Ash called, "Come on out, kids."

A flurry of whispers and giggles preceded three small bodies bursting into the room toward the foot of her bed. The older girl held the younger's hand, tagging along behind the boy, who looked like he might be nine or ten.

The boy had his eyes focused on Melody with a sort of fascination. "Are you going to be our aunt?"

She glanced at Ash, worry still clamped around her heart.

Ash merely raised his brows in reply, as if he had the same question.

She inhaled a shaky breath and licked her lips, wanting to avoid the question. Ash had promised to protect her and the child, but that meant little; her family made promises they couldn't or didn't keep all the time. Was Ash any different? Still, she already knew he was better than Brennan. "I think that's the plan."

A smile widened Ash's mouth, and relief flooded her so strongly it made her nauseous. Either that, or it was morning sickness. She gulped the sensation down. The last thing she wanted was to start dry-heaving in front of her potential new nieces and nephew. "Any chance Carmen has some saltines in the cupboard?"

"I'll get them!" shouted the older girl, and dashed off to the kitchen.

The boy stepped closer to Ash. "Uncle Ash, did you bring us anything?"

"Not this time, Rory. Sorry." He gave Melody a regretful look. "I usually bring them a treat when I visit."

"That's okay," Rory said. "You can bring something next time. Unless you're not leaving. Mom says you might stay now that you have a mate."

"Your mom's pretty smart. But don't tell her I said that." Ash faked a punch toward the boy's stomach, and Rory dodged, snorting with laughter.

Melody got up and headed to the bathroom, wondering what Ash meant. Was he planning to stick around and lead the pack like his sister wanted? That meant she'd be mated to an Alpha after all. Her chest felt tight, and she had to remind herself that Ash was nothing like Brennan. He'd be a kind Alpha, gentle yet strong. She could see it in the way he interacted with the kids.

When she returned, the littlest girl had pushed past her brother to stare at Ash, thumb in her mouth.

Ash tugged one of her stubby braids. "Hey, Rebel, I haven't seen you since you were a baby. Remember me?"

She shook her head, but climbed up onto his lap. He looked out-of-place sitting in the rocking chair cradling a toddler, but his tattooed arms and muscular frame obviously hid a softer side, one the kids could sense. He readjusted the small child and began rocking gently.

The older girl reappeared with a sleeve of crackers and a glass of water. "Here you go."

"Oh, what a good hostess!" Melody accepted them gratefully and tore open the package. "Thank you."

The girl beamed, climbing onto the mattress beside her. "My name's Roxie. I can baby-sit for you."

"You're not old enough, Roxie," said Rory.

"Am too!" Roxie turned to her older brother.

Sensing a fight, Melody stepped in. "I'll take all the help I can get, believe me."

Roxie sneered at her brother.

Rory lifted his chin, turning back toward his uncle. "Guess what, Uncle Ash? I made my first shift two weeks ago! If you stay, our wolves can hunt together."

Ash's eyebrows shot up. "Wow, you have your wolf? Are you old enough for that?"

The boy looked a long way from puberty, and a pang of jealousy rose inside Melody. It would've changed everything if she'd gotten a wolf at that age, before her father had died. *Don't be an idiot*, she told herself. If she'd gotten her wolf that young, she'd probably be a haggard, beaten omega, forced to marry Brennan the moment she turned eighteen and popping out her eighth kid by now.

Rory crossed his arms and stood taller. "Mom says I'm an early bloomer like my dad. My wolf has a white ruff like Mom's, though, not dark like his."

"My woof's going to be purple," said Roxie, rubbing her nose with the palm of one hand.

Ash laughed. "What does your mom say about that?"

"She says I can be anything I want."

A flicker of nostalgia made Melody sigh. Her father had encouraged her like this when she was Roxie's age, only she'd wanted her wolf to be orange.

A groggy Carmen emerged from the hallway wearing a red fleece bathrobe and slippers. "All right, kids. Stop pestering our guests and get ready for school."

"Aw, but we never get to see Uncle Ash," Rory whined.

"Don't worry, kiddo," Ash said. "I'll see you again soon."

Carmen raised her eyebrows but said nothing, following the two older children down the hall to the bedrooms. Rebel stayed planted on Ash's lap, cheek resting against his chest and thumb in her mouth. Her eyes blinked sleepily as he rocked.

Melody nibbled a cracker, wondering if he meant they'd be staying here at Carmen's a while longer. "Your sister's awesome. I like her."

He cocked an eyebrow. "Why's that?"

"We had a good talk last night. You should thank her."

"Uh, oh. For what? Besides letting us crash here, I mean."

The cracker she'd been chewing suddenly became too dry to swallow as Melody realized what she was about to tell him. She took a sip of water before looking at him over the rim of her glass. "She convinced me I should believe you about being mates. Called you a stand-up guy, to be exact."

Ash stopped rocking. "She did?"

Heart racing, Melody nodded.

A small voice inside her whispered, *ours.*

She froze, unsure what she'd just heard. *Is that you, wolf?*

Ash cocked his head, the question in his eyes mirroring her own. Had he sensed something, too? It would be a fairytale come true if her wolf had just been waiting for her to acknowledge her prince.

But nothing answered, and before she could ask Ash what he'd seen, Carmen reappeared. "You two want breakfast?"

Melody raised a cracker. "Roxie hooked me up."

Ash scrunched one eye. "You need something more substantial than crackers."

"Not unless you want to be holding my hair while I barf," Melody said. "Morning sickness."

Carmen gave her an understanding look. "I'll make some tea. That'll help." She nodded to Ash. "And for you, mister, I'm going to break out the bacon."

Making a yummy noise, Ash winked at Melody. "Carmen thinks bacon's unhealthy and should be reserved for special occasions. I guess you were right."

"About what?" Carmen asked.

He set Rebel onto her feet and stood. "That you think I'm a stand-up guy."

His sister rolled her eyes. "You shouldn't have told him that. Now every hunter in the state will be after him."

Melody frowned, confused. "Why?"

Carmen smirked. "His wolf's enormous head will make a legendary trophy mounted on their wall."

Ash guffawed and pulled his sister into an embrace that might've passed for a headlock. The surprised look on her face told Melody that didn't happen very often.

"Thank you, sis," he said. "For everything."

Carmen punched him lightly in the ribs and twisted free. "Whatever. I'm glad you're back."

Melody smiled. If nothing else, the trip here seemed to have repaired Ash's relationship with his sister. Finishing her cracker, she allowed herself a glimmer of hope that she might find a place in this family, too.

CHAPTER THIRTEEN

Following the path to the cabin was easier during daylight, sunlight making the bright clean snow sparkle between the tree trunks along the path. Ash angled the snowmobile around a log, enjoying the way Melody leaned back against his chest, although it made ignoring his hard-on difficult. He knew they still had a lot of things to talk about, and he would wait as long as it took for her to decide she was ready. She'd been abused by the people she trusted, and the last thing he wanted to do was anything that would frighten her away. So he willed his cock into submission and drove on.

Carmen had packed a few supplies and loaned them a sled to tow behind the snowmobile. He hadn't had time to consider food when he'd swept Melody away in his plane, and he'd hate to leave her just to make a run to

Anchorage for supplies. He also needed to pick up a job or two, but with the promise of Yates' marijuana income, Ash could wait a couple of days.

Right now, all he could think about was Melody.

He stopped the snowmobile to pick up her suitcase from the snow where he'd dumped it when he'd discovered her last night, then pulled under the portico. Cutting the engine, he stepped off the machine to give Melody standing room and opened the cabin door. Inside the mudroom, it smelled like home—a lingering presence of all the people who had lived here —even over the lingering odor of wood smoke. He opened the inner door, flicking on the light switch to bring a frosted glass and wood chandelier to life.

The cabin looked small from the outside, but with a high ceiling of varnished log beams, it was actually quite spacious. The back of the structure had been built into a hill that had housed the pack's original den, and each generation of his family had added onto the main cabin. There was a lot of history here, and he hoped Melody liked it.

Setting Melody's suitcase on the polished wood floor, he turned to find her inside, unzipping her coat. "Gonna grab the groceries," he said. "Be right back."

When he reappeared moments later, arms loaded with bags and boxes, she hadn't moved from the doorway, gaze on the natural slate alcove and wood stove. "I thought you said this place was rustic."

"Parts of it are," he said, toeing off his boots and stepping around the melting puddles of snow. "This is the newest section."

He nudged her to move all the way inside and closed the mudroom door behind them.

Melody took a few steps, running her fingertips along the nearby tongue-and-groove wall. She paused at the built-in bookshelf to scan a few titles, then turned her attention to the custom-made burled log furniture peppering the room.

He adjusted a carton of milk that was slipping from the crook of his elbow. "Let me put this stuff away, then I'll show you around."

"Here, I can help." Melody rescued the milk and a bag of chips from his other arm.

"Thanks." He headed toward a set of multi-paned glass double doors that led to the dining area.

Against the opposite wall under a bank of windows, a long table made of thick planks of polished birch was flanked by matching benches. He could remember many pack gatherings here as a child, the table laden with potluck dishes. Now its surface was covered in dust.

"This is huge," Melody said, brushing the table's corner with her fingertips.

"Mom used to love throwing parties." He smiled sadly. "Dad made her this table as a first anniversary gift. It seats fourteen, easy."

"If you don't mind me asking, what happened to them?" Melody asked, following him through the great room into the kitchen.

He set his things on the center island, his pulse increasing as long-buried emotions washed over him. "Mom died in a boating accident when I was in high school."

"And your dad?" Melody pressed.

That memory was harder, barbed with grief, regret, guilt. He stared at the walk-in freezer at the back of the kitchen, struck by how much the heavy door reminded him of prison. "I was in jail when he died."

"Oh, Ash, I'm sorry."

He forced his gaze away from the freezer and sorted through the groceries, opening and closing the cupboards to re-familiarize himself with the kitchen layout. Neat plastic containers filled the bottom shelves, labeled with things like rice and beans and flour, though most were nearly empty. Dad obviously hadn't been cooking much in the end.

"My parents were joint pack Alphas, but after Mom died, Dad said that leading the pack without her made him weary. I was the first pack member with a college degree, and on my way to becoming a lawyer. Dad planned on handing me the reins as soon as I passed the bar." He clenched his teeth and forced himself to meet Melody's gaze. "Mom's death broke his heart, but my mistake crushed what was left."

"I'm so sorry," Melody said softly. "I take it you didn't finish law school."

He laughed dryly. "Why bother? With a rap sheet for manslaughter, I'd be unlikely to attract many clients."

Her attention dropped to the tattoos on his arms. "To be honest, you don't look like a lawyer."

He smiled, knowing what she was thinking. "Long-sleeved dress shirts hide a multitude of sins."

"That makes sense. Is that why you became a bounty hunter?"

"No, I was hunting bounties for several lawyers during law school. I brought in people who skipped bail or had outstanding warrants, that sort of thing."

"Oh, right, you said you were after someone when that girl died..." her voice tapered off and she flushed, pressing her lips together.

"It's okay. We can talk about it if you'd like." Not that he wanted to, but it was bound to keep coming up if he didn't get it all out in the open.

She met his gaze and swallowed. "I don't really have any questions about that. It doesn't sound like it was your fault, just bad luck. But when we were with the kids, you said we needed to talk. Was there something specific?"

He put the eggs and butter into the fridge, eyeing a couple of his dad's Amstel Lights hiding behind a bottle of mustard. Damn, the nostalgia was hitting him hard. He shook it off and turned around. "My job takes me away from home, sometimes for weeks at a time. I want to be sure you have protection when I'm not around. You and the baby." He planted his hands on the island countertop, leaning into the cool granite surface for strength. "I'm not pressing you about becoming my mate—I want you to be safe whether you agree to or not. But if you're willing, my pack will accept you and keep you safe."

"Your pack—does that mean you're going to agree to be Alpha, then?"

Running a hand through his hair, he exhaled slowly. "That's a complicated question, but yes, I'm going to try."

She chewed her lip, looking uncertain. "You haven't talked to any of them in a long time. Are you sure they'll want anything to do with me?"

He grinned. "I'm not worried. Besides, Carmen's likely to throat-punch anyone who messes with you. If the pack won't look out for you on my behalf, they'll do it for her."

A smile blossomed on Melody's features. "I wish I had half her spunk."

He snorted. "You do, you just don't see it." Then he sobered again. "But I wanted to be sure you were on board with joining a new pack before I told Carmen my plan."

She took a deep breath. "I'm little more than property to my family's pack. I owe them nothing." She looked down at the countertop. "But I worry about my mom."

He took her hand and squeezed. "Once everything's settled here, I promise I'll check on her. Okay?"

The way her face lit up made him feel about ten feet tall. He would definitely have to find a way to free her mom from Brennan's clutches. Tugging Melody toward the dining room, he asked, "Ready to see the rest of the house?"

She nodded, interest flaring behind her eyes. "Okay."

Back in the great room, he pointed toward the short hallway with doors leading off from it. "There are five bedrooms, though the one at the back is more of a bunk room. Carmen and I used to have sleepovers in there."

Opening the doors one after another, he was relieved to find everything still in order. Each double bed was nestled in hand-sewn quilts, each room filled with warm gold light. Carmen's old room had been cleared of her things, but his childhood bedroom still had X-Men posters on the walls and his fly-tying kit set up on the desk. "This was my room growing up."

Melody pointed to a poster. "I had that same one! I had the biggest crush on Wolverine."

"You and everyone else." He wiggled his eyebrows. "Maybe I'll have to grow out my mutton chops."

She threw back her head and laughed in a way that made his inside thrum with joy.

They moved on to the master suite, and he set her suitcase on a chest at the foot of the bed. By now, his wolf was practically howling with impatience to claim both his mate and his territory, but Ash refrained from calling the room "ours." "This will be your room," he said. He planned on staying in his old room until Melody was ready to take that step. "The bathroom is through there."

Melody moved past him, drawing in a breath as she stepped through the bathroom doorway. "When you said your cabin was rustic, I pictured a one-room shack and an outhouse. This place is gorgeous."

He followed close behind, seeing everything with fresh eyes through her. The master bathroom was almost as large as the smallest bedroom, complete with Riverstone countertops and inlaid tile flooring.

"Oh, wow, is that a Jacuzzi tub?" she asked, gesturing to the double-wide sunken tub his parents had paid through the nose to have airlifted from Anchorage one summer.

He nodded. "Want me to run you a bath?"

"That sounds heavenly." She nodded vigorously. "I haven't had a bath in ages. My condo only had a shower."

Grinning at her delight, he turned on the water and rummaged through the towel shelves just inside the door. He found two glass jars half full of bath salts. "Mango or lavender?"

Melody was pulling her hair into a knot on her head, exposing the delicate line of her throat. She looked at him and spoke in a husky quality that made his dick jump to attention. "Which do you prefer?"

His heart stuttered, and he froze, wanting to pounce. "To smell on you, or to use myself?"

Her cheeks brightened, and she looked away. "I thought you might like to clean up a bit, too."

In two strides, he had her chin in his hand, turning her to face him. "I don't want any miscommunication, because it's all I can do to keep my hands off you. But I won't touch you without your permission. Are you inviting me to join you?"

She laughed shakily and ran a finger down the middle of his chest. How could she be so damn sexy and innocent at the same time? "I think I felt my wolf earlier, when we were with the kids."

His own wolf perked up. "Is that right? What did she feel like?"

Her hand slid up around the back of his neck and she lifted herself on her toes, bringing her lips to within millimeters of his. Sweet breath fanning his face, she said, "I can't be sure, but I think she was trying to tell me you're mine."

He closed the distance between their lips without hesitation.

$\mathcal{M}$elody had never felt this bold. This empowered. As if her wolf truly was on the verge of breaking free and only needed a nudge to release its bonds. She wanted to feel Ash's body against hers, skin to skin, to follow through on what could only be her wolf telling her what it wanted.

Ash swiped his tongue between her lips, sending chills across her entire body. She wrapped both hands over his shoulders and pulled herself closer.

He crushed her against him. His muscles felt like a wall of heated stone as his hands slipped down to cup her ass, grinding her against his very obvious arousal.

She relaxed, letting the moment carry them where it would. His kisses were making her feel delightfully woozy, drunk even. She'd love a bath, but if they ended up dropping to the floor and doing it in a frenzy on the tile, she certainly wouldn't mind. Ash had seemed frightening at first, but as she'd come to know him, she no longer feared him. He had a way of making her feel cherished and protected. She trusted him.

After a long moment, he pulled away. "I'm sorry. You wanted a bath."

"Screw the bath," she said, her voice husky with desire.

"I don't want to screw the bath." The light dancing behind his eyes made her giggle.

"Me either. But I would like to be clean." She dropped her hands from his neck and grabbed the hem of her shirt, pulling it up and over her head before eyeing the few inches of water in the tub. "The tub is huge. Filling it's going to take forever."

"Doesn't matter. Get in." He pulled his own shirt over his head and dropped his pants. The boxer briefs he wore strained over his erection.

Shyly, she stepped out of her jeans, self-conscious about her swollen middle, then turned around to strip out of her underthings. She felt his hands feather over her shoulders, and his breath heated the back of her neck as he steered her toward the tub.

She lowered herself into the huge basin, the shallow water warm as it lapped against her skin. Keeping her knees drawn up, she faced Ash.

He was naked now, and his shaft jutted from between his legs in a way that made her insides pulse with need. He was as long and thick as she'd imagined, and she knew her eyes must be round as twin moons as she dragged her attention to his face.

He didn't meet her eyes, stepping over the edge to join her and dropping to his knees. His gaze was riveted on where she hugged her knees. Slowly, he eased her hands free, fingers circling her wrists.

She kept her legs clamped together, a moment of hesitation washing over her. He'd asked for permission, but if she changed her mind now, would he stop? A part of her wanted to test it, to see if he was as trustworthy as she imagined.

The other part was terrified of his reaction if she did.

His hands released her wrists, and she held her breath, expecting him to force her knees apart, to take what he wanted, force her if necessary. It was what Brennan would've done. But Ash only ran light fingers down the insides of her calves to her ankles.

She shuddered, barely able to breathe. His touch drew tingling lines over her skin, and sensation rocketed up her legs to her core like an electric current.

Fingertips dipping below the level of the water to her instep, he drew upward again, trailing water as he rounded the curve of her knees to her thighs. Like magic, her legs seemed to part of their own accord.

His nostrils flared and his eyes flashed golden at the sight of her exposed pussy. Then his attention traveled up her torso to her face. Hands still on her knees, he paused, gaze locked with hers. "Is this still okay?"

He's asking permission. The realization empowered her. She nodded vigorously. She wanted him. Every long, hard inch.

With a growl of satisfaction, Ash pulled her upright, sliding her up to straddle his lap. Steamy warmth rose in clouds around them as he adjusted his hips, grazing his dick between her slick folds.

"You're so fucking hot," he said in a gravelly voice before running his tongue along her bottom lip.

The way he said it, with such awe, made her glow. She hadn't felt at all attractive lately, just bloated and scared. But here, in the warm embrace of the tub, in a cabin far away from everything she'd ever known, she felt like she finally had power. Control.

Exhaling a shuddering breath, Melody closed her eyes, hands resting lightly on his shoulders. She spread her legs wider, pressing his rock hard shaft along her slit.

A groan rumbled through him and he rolled his hips again, one hand palming her ass and shifting her over his heated shaft. His other hand slid up to fist into the hair at the base of her skull, pulling her head back gently before he covered Brennan's mark with his mouth. "I don't want to hurt you," he mumbled against her skin. "But I don't think I can take you without claiming you."

She tilted her head farther, every nerve vibrating with desire. If he marked her, she might feel the mate bond. Might sense her wolf. "Do it. I never want to think of anyone but you again."

His dick swelled against her entrance, probing without penetrating, and the points of his teeth grazed her skin.

Melody lifted off his lap and slid one hand between them to circle his girth and position the throbbing tip at the mouth of her entrance.

His breathing quickened, his hands on her hips gripping her firmly, on the verge of impaling her. Yet he restrained himself.

She smiled. He was letting her take the lead, have all the control. The sensation was exhilarating. Tilting her hips, she lowered herself an inch, taking him in, easing over his massive erection in a slow, delightful pressure.

He trailed kisses along her collarbone, bending to take one of her nipples into his mouth.

When he sucked hard, she cried out and arched her back, seating herself fully over his rock hard cock. The sudden fullness made her shudder with pleasure, tightening around him.

He grunted, hips pulsing upward in tiny thrusts that matched the way his tongue flicked over the swollen bud of her nipple. Entire body exploding with sensation, she gripped his shoulders hard, panting as her knees locked in place. The warm water sloshed in waves over her thighs as he fucked her from below.

His mouth left her nipple, and he gripped her neck, pulling her into a kiss. He was no longer asking for permission. He was demanding. Insisting. And she didn't mind one bit. His lips melded against hers, tongue plundering her mouth as he bucked.

Holy shit, whatever he was doing was making her insides go crazy. She moaned as he stroked her inner walls, the pressure in her core tightening. She was going to come. She *needed* to come. "Don't stop!"

He snarled and continued thrusting upward, entering her again and again with a powerful grace that made her eyelids flutter and the world spin.

Then, without warning, he flipped her onto her back. Water lapped at her sides and against the back of her neck, where his hand cradled her head against the sloped side of the tub as he thrust back inside her and continued pumping with a pace that left her panting. In and out he stroked, his tempo increasing until she felt like she could no longer breathe.

She clawed at his back and wrapped her legs around him as a tingling sensation filled her. "Ash!"

Ash gritted out something unintelligible as he slammed into her, hard. Once. Twice.

She burst into a million pieces.

His hips jerked, and his teeth clamped down over the mark on her shoulder. A distant pain sparked there, irrelevant amidst the cascade of pleasure. He slowed his rhythm to match her release, and warmth filled her, throbbing through her insides while stars sparked her vision.

When her body finished pulsing around him, she let out a long sigh, legs relaxing and falling from where she'd wrapped them around his hips.

Breathing hard, Ash lifted his weight off her, giving her room to push herself higher against the back of the tub. The water was midway up the sides now and luxuriously warm.

He kissed the curve of her neck where he'd marked her, then swiped a strand of wet hair from her cheek before kissing her temple, her jawline, her lips. "I didn't hurt you, did I? Or the baby? I'm sorry if I was too rough. I got a little carried away."

The sincerity in his gaze made her chest ache. He was worried about her. Cared about the baby, even. She smiled. "We're both fine."

A howl echoed somewhere outside, and unexpected terror spiked through Melody's chest. Had Brennan found her? If he found out what she'd just done, he'd murder them both. Melody started to rise, the air suddenly too thin to breathe.

"Don't get up. It's just Gregory. I'd recognize that howl anywhere." Ash pushed back on his knees, reaching around to turn off the faucet. "Guess word's getting out that I'm back. Stay here while I deal with him."

Melody breathed a sigh of relief and sank back into the warm water. Ash stepped from the tub and wrapped a towel around his waist. His gorgeous body made her pussy tighten with remembered bliss. He'd almost reached the doorway when he turned back with a grin, picked up the mango bath salt and sprinkled it over the surface around her, then disappeared through the doorway.

Steam infused the air with a fruity sweet aroma, and she closed her eyes, torn between wanting to meet Ash's pack and gratitude he was allowing her to hide. Carmen had been gracious, but the others in his pack might not appreciate an outsider hedging in on their Alpha. Especially one without a wolf.

She lifted her fingers to her shoulder and traced the tiny punctures from his teeth. The mark hadn't hurt like it had with Brennan, but it also hadn't transformed her as she'd hoped. Hadn't made her feel the mate bond or her wolf.

Refusing to allow sadness to ruin the moment, she reached for a bottle of shampoo and began massaging some into her hair. Even if she never felt the bond or her wolf, she'd just had the best sex of her life. She had a strong Alpha who believed she was his mate, whether she sensed the bond or not. And the chance of Brennan finding her here in the middle of nowhere was slim to none.

She might as well try to enjoy herself.

Melody gripped the snowmobile's handlebars, loving the sense of speed as she zoomed across the frozen lake ahead of Ash. Over the past week, she'd learned how to drive, and the Arctic gear and helmet Ash had dug up for her kept her toasty warm—a vast difference from the designer coat and boots she'd been wearing when she arrived. She liked to imagine this was what it would be like to run as her wolf. Free. Strong. Happy.

She glanced behind her toward Ash, keeping his distance on a second machine. He was a big part of that feeling. They'd spent their days either in bed or exploring his territory and meeting his pack. She loved hearing all the embarrassing stories about his childhood. Ash had a long history here, and she could tell he'd missed everyone and they'd missed him. He laughed at their ribbing and responded with stories of his own, both about them and himself.

The only time she'd worried about him blowing up had been when a woman laid into him for staying away for so long. But Ash had listened quietly, and when the woman finished, he'd given her hug and apologized. The pack obviously respected him, but not out of fear. Out of affection.

It was strange and wonderful at the same time. The way they'd welcomed her was even more surprising, especially since she'd not yet agreed to be his mate. The men grew protectively furious when Ash explained about Brennan, and the women were even planning a baby shower. Their welcome was a complete opposite to the resentment Melody had expected, and she felt free to be herself in ways she'd never dreamed of before now, even without a wolf to bolster her confidence.

Ahead on the bank where the creek emptied into the lake, she spotted a swelling of brown-tinged ice. They hadn't traveled this far before, but Ash wanted her to explore. *This is your land, too,* he'd told her. And some part deep inside her believed him.

Slowing her machine to a stop, she waited for Ash to pull up beside her and pointed at the discoloration. "That's overflow, right?"

He nodded, caution glinting in his eyes. "Yep. Steer clear."

The stories he'd told her about people falling through the ice made her nervous, so she turned to follow a set of snowmobile tracks that disappeared into the trees along the creek. She hit a soft patch of snow and accelerated, praying she wouldn't get bogged down. She'd already gotten stuck a few times and been grateful Ash was there to manhandle the heavy machine. He was so strong and always there the moment she needed him. Though she had yet to feel the mate bond, she knew he was the man for her.

The trail opened up on a clearing with a weathered gray cabin spouting smoke from the chimney. A haphazard pile of freshly split wood sat next to the door, and between the corner of the cabin and a nearby tree someone had strung a clothesline with tiny frozen onesies. *They have a baby!* Thrilled there might be another new mother to talk to, she pulled to a stop and cut the engine, sliding her leg over the seat and onto the packed snow outside the front door. She could hear Ash's heavier machine struggling through the trail's soft snow, but she was too excited to wait for him to catch up. Each household had welcomed her thus far, so she tromped toward the door. Why had no one mentioned there was a new baby?

Ash's machine burst from the trees, and he skidded to a halt between Melody and the building. He was off his machine in the blink of an eye. "Get back on your machine and go. Now."

Her stomach knotted. "What?" The wary lines creasing his eyes reminded her of Brennan when he was angry, and she backed toward her snowmobile. "Why?"

The cabin door swung open. A man with reddish curls poking from beneath his fleece cap stepped out.

Ash pivoted to face the man, both fists clenched at his sides.

The man's teeth showed slightly, but he looked more scared than ferocious, his freckled cheeks still hinting of baby fat. He mimicked Ash's posture. "What do you want?"

Heart hammering, Melody grabbed the handle of the snowmobile's pull start, yanking it to start the engine. The motor whirred and died.

"You're on Huntington land," Ash growled. "You need to move to the other side of the creek."

"We aren't causing any trouble," the man replied as Melody pulled the cord again.

"Doesn't matter," Ash said, his voice low. "You don't belong here, and I'll not have you claiming squatter's rights."

Her arm felt shaky and weak as she pulled a third time without success. What had she done? These people had a baby and now they were being forced to move. Ash never would've noticed if it hadn't been for her.

The smell of gas floated toward her, telling her she'd flooded the engine. *Shit! Now what?* She looked toward the standoff again. The stranger's eyes pulsed with the light of his animal on the verge of breaking loose.

From inside the house, a baby began to wail. Every nerve fiber in Melody's being flamed to life, and she rose from the seat. "Ash—"

A squat woman appeared in the doorway behind the man, holding a rifle pointed toward the ground.

It suddenly reminded Melody of her own mother. Dad had bought her a rifle, saying he wanted her to be able to protect herself. But Mom had been too timid to even touch it, insisting she didn't want a gun in the house. So Dad got rid of it.

This woman's posture made it obvious she had no such hesitation. "No one's used this cabin in years," the woman said, her voice firm. She looked no older than the redheaded man beside her. "Just leave us alone."

Ash raised his hands in a calming motion; even shifters weren't immune to bullets. He glanced over his shoulder at Melody. "Use my machine and go. Now."

Pack turf wars could get brutal, and Melody wanted to be anywhere but here right now. But something inside of her refused to leave. The baby continued to cry inside the house, making Melody jittery with the need to do something. If Ash hurt this couple, what would happen to the baby? Melody couldn't allow anyone to get hurt. *You're his mate. Calm him.* But she didn't know how.

Ash had returned his attention to the couple. "Are you from Quentin's pack?"

"He is." The woman tossed her chin in the man's direction.

The man scowled and turned to put his arm around the woman's shoulders, pulling her close. "Not anymore. Not if they won't accept my mate."

"Well, you're not in my pack, either." Ash pointed off to his left. "You need to go."

"What if they joined?" Melody blurted. "Our pack, I mean." Brennan always sought to strengthen his pack, by violence or by coercion. Ash didn't think like that, but more followers meant more power. This was an opportunity.

The woman's eyes widened. "You're the Huntington Alpha?"

Pale skin flushing beneath his freckles, the man dropped his arm from the woman's shoulders and stepped forward. "I'll swear my fealty right here and now, Alpha. Just let us stay."

The pressure in Melody's chest eased, and she smiled at Ash's stiff back. This would solve everything.

But Ash shook his head. "We don't have room for more members."

The man's face darkened, and even Melody could feel the air crackle with the shift coming over him. "Should've known you'd be a prejudiced fucker, too."

Ash planted one foot behind him and rolled his shoulders, as if bracing for the attack.

The woman looped her arm through her mates and pulled him back a step. "Shh, Matt, we talked about this. Don't do anything stupid."

The man's chest heaved with labored breathing, and Melody realized her own breath ached inside her chest. The baby's cries had taken on a rough tone, frantic. When Matt spoke again, his voice cracked. "It's the middle of winter and we have nowhere else to go. Please."

Melody's heart split open. Why was Ash being like this? She stared at his back, drawing up the courage to plead on the family's behalf. One step, then another, she moved to his side. Speaking in barely more than a whisper, she said, "Ash, they're not hurting anyone. And the baby… Could they at least stay until spring?"

He flicked a glance toward her, eyes haunted with something she didn't understand. Then he licked his lips and slowly unclenched his hands. "Until spring. Then you need to go. Agreed?"

A series of unreadable emotions flickered across the couple's faces before the man nodded. "We won't cause any trouble."

"Thank you," the woman added, her gaze falling gratefully on Melody before she turned to disappear inside.

The door shut, muffling the baby's crying, which ceased a moment later. Melody pictured the couple inside, comforting the child and each other as they contemplated their future.

Ash went to her machine and started the engine with one powerful pull. "Let's head back to the cabin."

Questions burned the back of her throat, but now wasn't the time to ask. Part of her felt exhilarated at having helped de-escalate a dangerous encounter. The other part worried there was something important she'd missed. Ash must have a reason for his actions. She just hoped he was willing to share them with her.

CHAPTER SIXTEEN

Ash followed Melody home, stewing over what he was going to do with the couple at the cabin. They hadn't directly told him their story, but he knew what it likely was; Quentin's pack didn't accept non-wolf shifters, let alone non-shifters, and he knew by her scent that the woman was still human. Even if she visited the Source with her mate and received an animal, there was no telling what it might be.

But that didn't mean he could simply adopt them into his pack. First of all, he knew nothing about them. Second, accepting new members would require him to call on his Alpha power, and that opened him up to mistakes. But revealing his vow not to use his power would make him seem weak. It might've even encouraged the boy to challenge him, and that was the last thing he wanted.

Thank God Melody had been there, or the entire situation could have ended in a blood bath. Letting them stay until spring was a temporary solution, but it would give everyone time to plan for alternatives. Hell, maybe he should take them to the glacier himself. If the woman got a wolf, they could go home to Matt's pack and be out of his hair for good.

Stopping his machine next to Melody, he told her to go inside while he refueled the machines. He knew he was going to have to tell her about his vow, but that didn't mean he was eager to do it. She was bound to think less of him. Perhaps even leave him. *You should've told her the truth in the beginning.*

He refilled the tanks and headed inside, hanging his gear on the wall and kicking his feet into a pair of slippers. Melody sat on the sofa in front of the wood stove, a steaming mug of cocoa cradled in her hands. She gestured with her chin to where a second mug sat on the coffee table next to a bottle of bourbon. "I made you coffee."

"Thanks." He sat next to her and poured a generous splash of alcohol into his mug. Maybe it would help him answer the question he knew was coming.

"Ash, I need a gun."

He blinked. That was the last thing he expected to hear, but after a puzzling moment, it made sense. She doubted his ability to protect her. He cleared his throat. "Do you know how to shoot?"

"No, but I can learn. You can't be around all the time, and I need a way to defend myself. Like that woman at the cabin."

He didn't mind Melody having a gun—in fact, he was ashamed he hadn't thought of giving her one himself. Carmen had owned a gun while she was pregnant and unable to shift. Melody was not only pregnant, she was still human. No wonder she felt a bond with the woman at the cabin. He asked, "Could you sense that she's human?"

Melody's eyes widened, and she shifted slightly away from him. "Is that why you wouldn't let them into the pack?"

"No, not at all."

"Then why?"

He took a deep breath and set his mug back on the coffee table before rising to put more wood in the stove. Melody remained silent while he composed his thoughts, and he was thankful for her quiet presence. When he turned around, he kept his face impassive, readying himself for rejection as he began. "I can't accept them into the pack unless I use my Alpha power, and I made a vow to never use it again."

She frowned, eyes roaming his face. "I understand your hesitation, but you agreed to lead the pack. How can you do that without using your power?"

"A good leader should be able to guide his people without magical coercion."

Her unblinking gaze remained fixed on him, mouth open slightly as she seemed to process what he'd said. "I knew you weren't like Brennan, but I never understood how much."

A boulder settled in his stomach. She believed her former Alpha was brutal, undefeatable. *She's worried I won't be able to protect her like he could.*

"I'll keep you safe, even without my Alpha power. I promise," he said hurriedly. "And I'll get you a gun, too. You're right, you shouldn't have to rely on me all the time."

She frowned and stood, coming to place a soft palm against his cheek. "You understand that I'm not asking because I doubt you, right? You were unbelievably strong today. It's easy to fall back on your magic to bend people to your will. It takes a lot more strength to treat them with respect."

Was that what he'd done? He wasn't entirely certain. The beast in him had railed to be let out, and the human side of him had wondered if he was being a coward.

We kept our mate safe, his wolf reminded him, the urge for blood already forgotten. It was the human side of him that couldn't forgive. Couldn't forget.

Pressing a kiss into Melody's palm, he led her back to the sofa. "I just hope they respect me back and leave come spring."

"Couldn't they be part of the community without joining the pack?" She sat down, facing him slightly. "Humans live together all the time without magical bonds. If everyone gets along, what's the harm?"

Ash ran a hand through his hair. "I don't want to give them false hope about joining the pack."

"It would be nice to have another new mom nearby," Melody mused, rubbing a hand over her abdomen. "Since they were kicked out of his pack, I bet they don't have much of anything for the baby. I'd like to help them."

He frowned. "You don't even know their names, Melody."

"So? She's a desperate mother, just like me. Maybe I could invite her to my baby shower and share a few things."

It made sense for her to desire friends with common interests, but this might be pushing the limits of what his pack could accept. "Mm. Not sure how Carmen will feel about it."

"It can't hurt to ask her." Melody picked up her cocoa.

He opened his mouth, searching for another argument, but couldn't find one. Assuming she could convince Carmen to agree, the rest of the pack would accept the newcomers without question. This could be a way around using his Alpha power.

Our mate is wise, his wolf thought with approval.

He shook his head in admiration. "All right. If Carmen agrees about the baby shower, we'll try it your way."

Smirking, she leaned back against him. "Excellent. I'll talk to her tonight."

He put an arm around her shoulders. "Keep this up, and the pack might decide you make a better Alpha than I do."

She laughed, the warm, rich sound filling him with contentment. "Well, they do say the man is the head of the family, but the woman is the neck. He can only look where she turns him."

Chuckling, he kissed the top of her head. This conversation hadn't gone at all as he'd expected. Melody had not condemned him for refusing to use his power. And not only that, she was willing to help him find ways around it. To lead the pack as partners the way his parents had. All that was left now was to get her her wolf.

CHAPTER SEVENTEEN

Surprised at how heavy the shotgun was, Melody turned it over in her hands. Ash was pointing out the various parts and reiterating the need to keep her finger away from the trigger until she was ready to shoot. The gun had belonged to Carmen's ex, and when Ash had asked if they could borrow it, Carmen said she was happy to get it out of her house.

"Here, let me show you how to reload." Ash demonstrated how to push a cartridge into the slot.

Melody repeated the motion, filling the magazine, then followed his instructions to rack a round into the chamber, pleased she at least had this part down.

The whine of an approaching plane drew her attention, and she looked up to see a small aircraft banking over the lake, dropping altitude with clear intent to land.

Her chest tightened. There hadn't been a single plane in the sky the entire time she'd been here. *Brennan found me.*

"It's the mail plane," Carmen said from where she was stacking wood next to the house. She winked. "Probably full of baby gifts. I'll run over and meet it."

Ash gripped the gun barrel as if about to take it away. "Melody, are you paying attention?"

"Uh, yes." Melody gulped.

"Take it easy, Ash," Carmen said as she passed them on the way to the snowmobile shed. "The girl has reason to be on guard."

"This thing isn't a toy," he gritted.

Carmen punched him in the shoulder. "And she's not a child. Melody, if you ever need to escape this asshole, the mail plane can sometimes squeeze in a passenger, too."

Ash scowled in his sister's direction as she started her snowmobile, but then turned back to Melody. "I'm sorry I snapped. You understand how dangerous this is, though, right?"

"I'll be careful. I promise." The last thing she wanted to do was accidentally hurt or kill someone.

He nodded and stepped back. "All right. Let's keep going. Put on your ear protection and take a shot at the target."

Settling the butt of the gun against her shoulder like Ash had showed her, she looked down the barrel toward the empty can sitting on a snowbank.

"Remember to breathe," Ash said, voice muffled through her earmuffs.

Melody exhaled a frosty gust of air and squeezed the trigger. The gun slammed into her shoulder with excruciating force, rocking her backward a step. "Ow!"

"Awesome!" Ash said.

"I hit it?" The can no longer sat on the snowbank, and it took her a second to spot it several feet away in the snow.

"Sure did. Now do it again."

Teeth clenched against the bruise forming on her shoulder, she lifted the gun again, took aim at a second can—and missed. Her shoulder felt like someone had knocked it out of its socket, and her ears rang despite the ear protection.

Carmen returned with several boxes strapped to her snowmobile.

Ash called, "Need a hand?"

"I got it."

He turned back to Melody. "Remember to settle the butt into the pocket of your shoulder. And try not to anticipate the recoil. It's affecting your aim."

"Easy for you to say. You're not the one getting repeatedly punched." She placed a hand over her twitching abdomen. "And now the baby has hiccups."

Concern filled his gaze. "We can stop whenever you want."

But Melody was determined to hit the target at least one more time.

Carmen came back outside and watched her miss a few more shots. "My ex used to say, 'You're a willow branch, not a wall,'" she said, mimicking a deep, nasal voice. "Drove me crazy, but it helped."

Squinting against the dazzling sun bouncing off the snow, Melody tried to imagine herself as a willowy sapling. She pulled the trigger. The butt jerked back against her shoulder again, but this time she rolled with it. The can flew into the air and landed in the snow several feet away.

"Woo hoo!" cheered Carmen.

Melody grinned. "Your ex might've been a bastard, but he must've known how to shoot."

"I think you're getting the hang of it." Ash nodded and headed over to put the targets back in place.

The buzz of the mail plane taking off sawed through the air, and Melody lowered the shotgun to watch the small craft disappear over the tree line. *He can't find me.* With no previous connection to Ash or this pack, there was zero reason Brennan would ever think to look for her here.

But it was hard to shake off her wariness.

Turning to let the sun warm her front, Melody dug in her coat pocket for the extra rounds. Neither Carmen nor Ash had bothered wearing coats today, but her nose felt tingly with cold, and she felt like she constantly needed to rotate to keep the shady side of her body thawed.

A snowmobile approached, and Melody recognized the man as one of the pack members she'd met briefly a few days ago. She couldn't recall his name.

"Hey, Ash, I need to talk to you!" the man shouted over the thrumming motor, brown hair flopping over one eye as he came to a halt.

Ash's smile faded. "I'll be right back, ladies."

The two men moved around to the other side of the house.

"Who is that guy again?" Melody asked.

"Yates." Carmen's lips curled a little. "I'm glad Ash is back to handle him."

"Wonder what he wants?"

"Who knows?" Carmen shrugged. "Just steer clear of him if you can. He's a loose cannon."

Nodding, Melody wondered if that was why Ash had seemed to want to keep the man away from her; he was the only person Ash had been hesitant about, other than the couple at the creek. Which reminded her… "Hey, Carmen, can I ask a favor?"

"No."

Melody stiffened. What had she done wrong? She raised her eyes to meet her sister-in-law's and realized to her relief that Carmen was teasing by the grin curling her lips. *She's treating me like she treats Ash. Bantering like a sibling.* It made her want to tear up. Instead, she scrunched her nose and sassed back, "Well, I'm going to, anyway. I have a friend I'd like to invite to the baby shower."

Carmen pursed her lips and cocked her head. "I thought no one knew you're here."

"I just met her. She has a baby, too." Melody smiled brightly, hoping a cheerful attitude about this would win Carmen over.

Questions filled Carmen's eyes. "There aren't any new babies in the pack."

"We met the couple staying in the cabin by the creek."

Carmen did a double take, then shook her head. "Oh, hell no. They belong to Old Man Quentin's pack."

"No, they don't. At least, not anymore." Melody toggled the gun's safety before resting the butt on the ground. "It sounds like Quentin banished them because the woman's human."

"Well, they need to leave." Carmen crossed her arms. "Unless they want to join our pack, of course."

Melody considered telling Carmen about the man's offer to swear fealty—but then she'd have to explain why Ash had declined, and he didn't seem to want anyone else to know. *Ash will tell his sister when he's ready*. "I convinced Ash to let them stay until spring. They're not hurting anything."

"Letting them stay is a mistake. It sets a precedent. Before you know it, every lone wolf in the territory will be on our doorstep for handouts. And if they're not bound to our pack, they don't owe us shit. Besides, I know this guy's type. All goo goo over his kid for the first few months, but eventually, he'll abandon his family and go back to his pack."

Melody bristled, but calmed herself down. Tension and force were the last things that would work against Carmen's strong personality. "You know nothing about him. Give him a chance. They're barely more than kids themselves."

"I don't like it." Carmen's scowl deepened.

Melody let out a breath. Ash had been right—Carmen would not be easy to bring around. But that didn't mean Melody had to give in, either. "You begged Ash to come back and be Alpha." Her heart stuttered at her bold words, but she held her ground, staring the woman straight in the eye. "If you want that to happen, then let him do his job. Okay?"

Something in Carmen's gaze shifted, a begrudging acceptance, and she nodded. "Fine. But the moment he leaves her or there's trouble, I'm ready to step back in."

The adrenaline left Melody in a rush, and the gun suddenly felt ten times as heavy as before. "I think I'm done practicing for today." The baby shower wasn't for another few weeks, so she had time to soften Carmen's heart on the matter. "My shoulder is killing me."

"Yeah, I remember that part. Never understood why my ex enjoyed collecting guns he then had to take out and shoot."

Hoping to break the sour mood their discussion had created, Melody said, "Maybe to compensate for a small penis?"

Carmen guffawed. "Probably! Come inside and I'll make us some lunch."

"Ash! Carmen's going to feed us!" Melody called as they rounded the cabin, knowing he wouldn't pass up his sister's cooking.

Yates stalked past them, nodding curtly before he climbed onto his snowmobile and zipped away. Ash's face seemed creased with worry.

"Everything okay?" Melody asked at the same time Carmen said, "What's going on with Yates now?"

Ash forced a smile and ran his fingers through his hair. "Nothing. He just reminded me the mortgage is due. I need to head to Anchorage tomorrow and make a payment."

Melody frowned, heart sinking. She remembered he'd said he sometimes needed to leave for extended periods. "How long will you be gone?"

"I'm not sure. A few days, at least."

Carmen put an arm around Melody's shoulder. "Don't worry. Now that you're here, he won't be able to stay away like he used to."

Melody side-hugged her back. "Can we take a raincheck on lunch?" She stepped away to take Ash's hand. "I'd like to spend some time with Ash before he leaves."

"Of course! You two go have fun. And feel free to come over while he's gone."

Ash pulled Melody toward the snowmobiles. "Thanks, Carmen."

Melody followed Ash down the trail toward home, her heart heavy. *Guess the honeymoon's over.*

As Ash packed a duffel bag, he tried not to be angry—at himself, at Yates, at the world in general. Yates's pot deal had fallen through, and the payment on the mortgage was already overdue. *Should've known better than to trust everything would be okay.* But it had been so nice to forget his financial troubles and focus only on Melody.

At the moment, she sat curled up in the plush armchair next to the wood stove in the bedroom. "I'm going to miss you."

"I love hearing that," he said, tossing socks and underwear into the bag. "I'll hurry, I promise. If you're lonely, you can stay with Carmen. She'd be happy to have you."

"No, Carmen has enough on her plate. I'll be fine." She held up the skein of purple yarn and knitting needles she'd found in one of the bedrooms. "I'm going to figure out how to make a baby hat and watch chick flicks on DVD."

Smiling, he moved over to plant both hands on the armrests of her chair and gave her a resounding kiss. "You're amazing. I'm not leaving until dawn, though. Need anything before I go?"

She ran light fingertips down his neck to his chest. "A few more kisses would be nice."

He needed no further encouragement. Tossing his bag to the floor, he took her to bed and made love to her until darkness blanketed the sky. She fell asleep in his arms, and he stroked gentle fingers over the swell of her abdomen as he thought about going back to work. He might not be excited about leaving, but he'd do what he needed to make their lives here happy.

The moment dawn's purple light streaked the sky, he rose, made a pot of coffee, and left Melody a love note in the fridge next to her favorite yogurt. If he put in a long day, he might be able to bring in a bounty or two, run payment to the bank, and head home tomorrow.

When he arrived at his plane, he discovered Yates sitting on the dock. "Mind if I come along? I'm going to sell what I have on the street. At least make some cash that way."

Ash wasn't thrilled about the idea of taking this weed business to the next level, but Yates was going to do it whether he helped or not, so he shrugged. "Sure. But I'm not bailing you out if you get caught. And I can't say for sure how long I'll stay in Anchorage."

"That's all right. I need to drown my sorrows in a few lap dances." Yates tossed a backpack reeking of weed behind the seats and climbed in.

A quick forty-five minutes later, they touched down in Birchwood and they tossed their bags into the bed of his pickup.

Yates asked, "Mind dropping me off downtown? "

"You drive. I need to make some calls."

By the time they reached the city, Ash had a list of bounties to track and papers to serve. None offered a big payout; he was going to have to finish several to earn enough money for the mortgage.

With a heavy sigh, he let Yates out and headed to an Indian restaurant in midtown where one bounty had last been seen. This was going to be a long week.

It took Ash three days to collect half of what he needed for the mortgage. Then Yates called to tell him he'd not only avoided jail, he'd found a buyer. Together they had enough money for the mortgage and to buy supplies and refuel the plane.

Things were looking up.

As they headed back toward Birchwood, the afternoon sun in his truck's rearview mirror, his phone rang.

He tapped the speaker. "Ash here."

"Hey. Where are you?"

Ash didn't recognize the man's voice, but he had a lot of contacts. "I'm in Anchorage. Who's this?"

A muffled scratching, like the person was shifting the phone around. "It's Talvin. How long are you in town? I need your help on a case."

Talvin? He scowled at the dirt-caked tail lights ahead of them. It wasn't unheard of for bounty hunters to join forces and split the money, but it wasn't as if he had a working relationship with the fox shifter. *Maybe he's still on Melody's trail.* The thought sent a chill down Ash's spine. "What case?"

"It's easy money once I get your help. Meet me at the Kaladi Brothers coffee shop on Tudor around four and I'll tell you."

He had no desire to work with Talvin, but if the fox shifter was still working for Brennan, it would be good to find out what he knew. He glanced at the clock on his dashboard—almost an hour to kill before the meeting. "Fine, see you then."

Yates shot him a questioning look. "What's up?"

"I have one more thing to do." He shoved the phone into the truck's cupholder and took the off-ramp to head back toward town. He'd already warned the pack to be on the lookout for anyone suspicious, so he explained about Talvin's involvement.

"Can I help?"

"I'm just after information. Shouldn't take too long."

Yates nodded and settled back against the seat. "Gotcha."

They pulled into the parking lot of the strip mall with the coffee shop and headed inside, immediately enveloped in the scent of freshly roasted coffee and the hum of conversation. A line of people stretched along the pastry cases in front of the register, and the tables out front were full. Yates stood in line for coffee while Ash stepped around the corner to a large alcove holding more tables, looking for a spot to wait.

A familiar weasel-like figure sat hunched over a to-go cup while tapping into his phone, his back against one of the burnt-orange walls. *Talvin.*

Ash could get this meeting over with and go home. He edged between the crowded tables and stopped at the chair across from the man. "Hey."

Talvin startled, nearly dropping his phone. "You're early." His gaze flicked to a nearby table where a pair of teenage girls had their heads together, looking at a phone and giggling.

"So are you." Ash pulled out a chair and sat. He disliked putting his back toward the door, but hopefully this meeting wouldn't last long.

The fox shifter's sweat smelled nervous over the bitter aroma of coffee. Not surprising, since the last time they'd met, Ash hadn't exactly been friendly. "One sec," said Talvin, finishing whatever he was doing on his phone.

"I'm a busy man, Talvin. What do you want?"

Setting the phone aside, Talvin licked his lips nervously and cocked his head, affecting a constipated smile. "Whatcha working on now?"

Ash thrust out his chin. "I'm not here to talk about my work. You said you have an offer."

Talvin's throat bobbed. "Er, yeah." He rubbed a hand over the back of his neck. "It's, um, about that last bounty. You know, the one at the pawn shop?"

So this is about Melody. Ash leaned forward. "Go on."

"The reward's still out for her. It's gone up, in fact."

"Okay." Ash tilted his head. "What's it got to do with me?"

The sound of chairs moving behind Ash's shoulder drew Talvin's gaze. Ash glanced around. The two girls at the table behind him were leaving. A man in a business suit plopped his computer case down before they'd cleared their cups. At the register, a pair of police officers were looking their way.

A funny tingle ran down Ash's spine. He didn't like cops, but he'd learned that acting guilty was a sure way to attract attention, so he turned back around.

Talvin had risen and was now blocking Ash's chair with his fists clenched at his sides. "I want what you owe me."

"What?" Ash scowled.

"You heard me, asshole. You cost me a lot of money."

The man had to be referring to the bounty on Melody. It was the only thread they had in common. But why would he think he could bully Ash for money?

Ash stood, elbowing Talvin out of his way. "I have no idea what you're talking about."

Then the fox did the most unexpected thing. He chested up to Ash. "Don't shove me! You're a cheat and a liar! Now pay up."

The buzz of voices stilled as everyone's attention turned toward them. Instinct swelled inside Ash, a need to command this fool to stand down. His wolf wanted to tear the man's face off, but he had to remain calm. "Get the fuck out of my way," he growled.

Then Yates came out of nowhere. He grabbed Talvin by the shoulder and threw a punch against his nose. Blood spurted over the wooden chairs and tables.

"What the hell, Yates?" Ash said. Starting a fight was exactly what he was trying to avoid.

"It's a set up, Ash. Go home. Now." Yates swung an uppercut against the fox shifter's jaw.

People were shouting, chairs scraping. The police officers Ash had seen earlier swooped in, wrestling Yates to the ground.

"Not him." Talvin clutched his bleeding nose. "The other one!"

Ash backed up a step. Two. Then turned and bolted for the door. *A set up*. Talvin was trying to get Ash thrown in jail. Why? And how had Yates known? He didn't have time to question. All he knew was he had to get home.

Melody was in trouble.

CHAPTER NINETEEN

Melody had told Ash she'd be fine alone at the cabin, but after two days of knitting slightly uneven baby hats, she changed her mind. She missed Ash painfully, and his nightly phone calls did little to soothe the ache. She missed Ash painfully, and knew it had to be the mate bond. Part of her was glad she could finally feel it, yet another part of her resented the pain, resented his absence.

She needed to do more than sit around by herself, moping.

Gathering up the baby hats and one of the many frozen casseroles the pack had given them as welcome gifts, she started her snowmobile and headed for the remote cabin where the couple with the baby were staying. Food was always a suitable gift, right? She didn't know why she had such a powerful urge to help them, but it couldn't be denied.

At the cabin, no one answered her knock. Stepping away, she looked around. Different clothing hung from the drying line, and smoke came from the chimney. She knocked again, then pressed her ear to the door, but couldn't hear anyone. "Hello? It's Melody. We met the other day. I've brought you some welcome gifts!"

Still no answer.

Uncertain if there was truly no one home or if she was being ignored, she left the gifts perched against the front door and headed to Carmen's. She hoped someone was home there.

She parked her machine near the shed, then knocked, suddenly feeling a little awkward about stopping by without warning. Rory answered. "Hi, Aunt Melody."

She stepped inside, and the delicious scents of garlic and toasted sesame oil washed over her. Her mouth immediately began to water. "Oh my God, what is your mom cooking?"

"I dunno. Weird stuff." Rory left her to take off her things, shouting, "Mom! Aunt Melody's here!"

Melody made her way to the kitchen to find Carmen pouring sauce over crispy bites of chicken. It looked and smelled exactly like the sesame chicken from

Melody's favorite Chinese restaurant. "Is that what I think it is?"

Carmen laughed. "I heard it was your favorite. I was going to bring it by and see how you were doing, but now that you're here, we can all eat together." She picked up the platter. "I swear, if I never had adults over, all we'd eat around here would be boxed mac and cheese and hot dogs. Will you grab the rice please?"

Stomach grumbling in anticipation, Melody picked up the rice cooker and carried it into the dining room after Carmen.

"Kids, come eat!" Carmen yelled, setting the platter on the beat-up wood table. She pointed to a spot at the far end. "Go ahead and sit down. I'll grab some plates."

The patter of small feet approaching at a run preceded all three children pushing into the dining room. They climbed into their respective chairs and looked warily at the golden brown lumps of chicken.

Rory wrinkled his nose. "What is this?"

"It's sesame chicken," Melody replied, helping Rebel into her booster chair. "You're going to love it."

"I don't like it," said Roxie, crossing her arms. "I want peanut butter."

"Me too," said Rebel, mimicking her older sister's crossed arms.

Carmen returned and started setting out plates. "Everyone tries one bite."

Melody opened the rice cooker and scooped out a fragrant mound of rice. "Do you kids like rice?"

"Yes, with butter!" Roxie jumped from her chair and disappeared into the kitchen.

Carmen sighed and shouted after her retreating body, "You only get butter after you try the chicken."

The perfectly crisp breading soaked in savory sauce nearly made Melody swoon as she chewed her first bite. "I've never eaten anything so delicious in my life."

"See? You should try it," Carmen said, trying to convince a tight-lipped Rebel to open her mouth.

Rory picked up a hunk with his fingers and licked it. "It's kinda sweet."

Melody was savoring a second bite when the buzz of an airplane overhead made her look up at the ceiling. She gulped down the bite and stood. "Ash!"

Had he tried to call? Cell service out here was spotty, and she hadn't been paying attention to her phone. She raced for her coat and boots, bursting out the door and into the cold winter air.

It had to be him.

"Aunt Melody, wait for me!" Roxie rushed after her, fighting to zip her coat as Melody climbed onto her snowmobile. "I want to come with you." The little girl's pleading eyes were impossible to deny.

Melody had never taken a passenger before, but she'd watched Carmen tote kids around. It didn't look hard. She glanced at Carmen standing in the cabin door. "Is that all right?"

"Go on." Carmen waved them off.

"All right, hop on," Melody told Roxie.

The girl climbed on behind. Melody had learned from the children that "only babies rode in front." When she'd asked Ash about her first ride with him, he'd flushed and admitted it had been an excuse to hold her. *God, I'm so glad he's back.* She was not looking forward to when his jobs took more than a few days.

With the girl clinging to her coat, Melody nudged the throttle, putting the machine into motion down the trail to the lake. Scanning the overcast sky, she didn't see the plane, but the sound of the engine had dropped an octave, like it was already taxiing after landing. Careful not to dump Roxie off the back, she followed the trail through the trees, picking up speed once she turned onto the frozen lake. The shape of a plane sat at the dock, and her heart thrilled with anticipation. But as she drew near, she realized it wasn't Ash. This plane was bigger and yellow, not blue. Her heart fell. It was probably another mail plane. Carmen had complained about the last mail plane bumping packages, so another one must've come to drop them off.

She slowed as she caught sight of two men tying the plane to the dock. With Roxie on board, she couldn't take packages with her, but she could let the pilot know someone would be along to collect everything soon. One man straightened and turned toward her.

Her sesame chicken rose in her throat.

She recognized his face.

He was from her pack.

From Brennan's pack.

Adrenaline surged through her, and she yelled over her shoulder at Roxie, "Hang on!"

Turning the snowmobile in a wide arc, she leaned into the curve. She had to get away. Find safety. Roxie's arms gripped her tighter, but the girl would fall off if Melody accelerated too fast. She squeezed her elbows against her sides, over the top of Roxie's hands to help secure her.

As they picked up speed, despair laced through her veins. Ash had made her feel safe, yet she'd known Brennan would find her, even all the way out here in the wilderness. She never should've let her guard down. Now the gun was all the way back at her cabin, and the plane was between her and it.

Carmen and the rest of the pack would try to defend her, but Melody couldn't allow Brennan to hurt them. There'd been at least two of Brennan's betas at the plane, and there were likely more, plus Brennan himself. If Melody didn't stop them, there would be bloodshed.

And the only way to do that was to surrender herself to the monster.

Her gut felt hollow as they neared the turnoff to Carmen's place. She couldn't lead Brennan back there. Perhaps if she drew him away, she could keep the pack out of it. She slowed to a stop. Roxie could make it home from here on foot.

"Run home, Roxie." Melody pried the girl's hands from her coat. "Tell your mom to stay inside and lock the doors."

"What's wrong, Aunt Melody?" Roxie climbed off. "Are those men bad?"

"Yes, but I'll take care of them. Go on, quickly."

The child's terrified gaze swept past Melody to something behind them.

Twisting, Melody spotted a familiar black wolf pounding toward them, bared fangs gleaming. *Brennan.*

Her chest felt too tight to breathe. Two more big wolves trailed close on his heels. "Shit. Go, Roxie. Run!"

The girl turned and bolted down the trail into the trees.

Melody gunned the throttle, sending the machine forward with enough force to almost make her lose her grip on the handlebars. Snow churned behind her as she plowed through fresh snow, planning to lead the pack away from occupied territory. She glanced behind her to make certain they were following her.

One wolf had split off to follow Roxie.

"No!"

She cranked the handles around, nearly tipping over on herself, and headed straight for the oncoming pack. She might not have a gun, but that didn't mean she was helpless. She'd run each of them over with this machine if that's what she had to do.

Aiming straight at Brennan, she gritted her teeth and maxed the throttle. The machine roared, drowning out the pulse thundering through her ears.

She locked eyes with the man who had beaten and raped her, and screamed into the wind, "I'm coming for you, asshole!"

Cold air made tears blur her vision, but she kept going, keeping him in her sights. She was going to end this, one way or another.

The remaining wolf broke off to flank her, his clawed feet sinking into the snow.

Just focus on Brennan. He was the key. If she eliminated him, the others would likely retreat.

Black fur filled her vision. She braced for impact.

At the last moment, Brennan bunched into a leap that carried him over her head. His claws snagged into her hat as he passed, yanking it from her head and nearly pulling her off the machine. She clung to the handlebars for dear life, fingers painfully tight.

Damn it. Now Brennan and his crew were behind her. She had to reach them before they hurt Carmen and the kids. Letting off the throttle, she circled back, determined to face him head-on. Instead, she came face to face with the beta who'd flanked her, a red and black wolf with patchy fur.

Before she could gun the throttle, something slammed into her side, wrenching her off her seat.

She landed hard, breath knocked from her ribs. Her machine continued forward without her, unmanned. Blinking, she rolled onto her back. A shadow blotted out the gray sky overhead, and a giant, slavering wolf straddled her, panting carrion breath into her face.

Brennan.

Hot saliva dripped from his tongue.

He lingered there for a heartbeat. Two. She was sure he was going to tear her throat out.

Then, in a shower of sparks bright enough to make her wince, he shifted to human form. Brennan rose, naked and hairy and obviously aroused by the chase. "I think we should play this game more often, mate. You're usually such a wet blanket."

Bile rose into her throat. "You're not my mate."

His gaze slid to her belly, nostrils expanding. "You're carrying my child. Your grandfather will be delighted."

"I'm not going back." She pushed herself upright. "This is my home now."

A scream cut through the frigid air from the direction of Carmen's house, followed by a wolf's howl. Dread clamped down on her gut.

Brennan's lips split into a malicious grin. "Oh, we're going to have so much fun."

CHAPTER TWENTY

Ash reached the Birchwood Airport and brought the truck to a skidding halt near his plane. A man in a tan coat and jeans looked up from the open engine compartment, then bolted, leaving behind what looked like parts from Ash's engine scattered on the ground. The smell of fox shifter drifted through his heat vents.

"What the fuck?" Ash snatched his keys from the ignition and launched from the truck, giving chase around the corner of a hangar. The man had disappeared among the cars and planes parked along the side of the building, but Ash could still follow him by the stale scent of cigarettes and fox shifter sweat.

Just past the corner of the next hangar, he spotted the man trying to crouch behind a dumpster and put on a burst of speed. Tackling the guy, he flipped him over to get a look at his face. "What the hell did you do to my plane?"

The man cringed against the snowy pavement. "I'm sorry, I'm sorry."

Ash grabbed his throat and squeezed. "I don't want your worthless apology. Tell me what you did."

"I pulled the alternator belt," the man choked.

"Why?"

The man squirmed, the reek of sweat growing stronger. "I was hired to keep you grounded."

Ash squeezed harder. "By who?"

"I'm not sure," the man gasped. "Talvin made the deal. All I know is I'll get an easy grand for disabling your plane."

Talvin must've put two-and-two together after Ash hadn't collected the bounty on Melody. He was a better investigator than Ash had given him credit for.

Ash jerked the man to his feet. "Fix my plane."

"Okay, okay." The man stumbled ahead, glancing over his shoulder toward Ash until they reached the plan. He began putting pieces back into the engine.

"You'd better make sure everything is perfect," Ash said, breathing down the back of the man's neck. "Because you're coming along for the ride."

The man blanched and nodded.

While he worked, Ash tried Melody's cell, but got her voicemail. Not surprising; reception was shitty out at the cabin. Still, a feeling of dread crept through his gut. He left a quick message, then texted, *Hide. He's found you.* Next, he called the rest of the pack, hoping someone would pick up. Not a single answer. He texted them as well. *Protect Melody. She's in danger.*

Frustrated and worried, he paced for what felt like forever, continuing to dial numbers while the mechanic worked. The moment the guy closed the engine compartment, Ash shoved him in the passenger seat, grabbed some zip ties and bound the guy's hands and feet.

Ash pushed the Cessna to its limits, and they reached the lake barely thirty minutes after takeoff. But the mechanic at least valued his own skin, and they remained airborne. As he came in for a landing, he spotted an unfamiliar plane parked at the dock. His pulse raced. It had to be Brennan or his cohorts. How long had they been here? There was no traffic on the lake, and several lazy plumes of smoke from the scattered cabins made it seem like nothing was amiss.

Had anyone gotten his texts? He checked his phone, but he'd worn down the battery trying to call out. *Damn it.*

Bumping down on the ice, he taxied to a stop next to the other plane. It had been tied to the dock, and no one appeared to be nearby. Both boots and paws had trampled the snow around the plane. *Paws.* Coming to a full stop, he cut the engine and jumped from the cockpit.

"Hey, what about—?" the fox shifter called from the plane, but was cut off as Ash slammed the door. The guy would be fine. Right now, Ash needed to get to Melody.

He scouted the area around the other plane, picking up the scent of several unfamiliar wolf shifters, including the distinct smell of an Alpha. It had to be Brennan. Every hair on Ash's body stood on end, and his wolf surged inside him, demanding to be let free. Ash tore off his clothing and shifted.

Lowering his nose to the ground, he picked up the Alpha's scent heading off toward Ash's cabin with two other wolves. Ash bolted in that direction. If Brennan so much as spoke a mean word to Melody, Ash would rip out his tongue.

He was just over halfway home when a howl rose from the direction of Carmen's place. He recognized the voice of his eldest pack member, Gregory.

He raised his muzzle and howled in return, calling back. But a mere howl couldn't transmit the urgency he was feeling. Tension thrummed through his blood. As Alpha, he had the power to talk silently with his pack when they were in range, but he'd never used it. If there was ever a reason to break his vow, this was it. *Melody's worth it.*

Summoning his power, he found the link in his mind and called out to Gregory. *I need you with me now!*

The older wolf responded, *I can't. Brigit's torn up pretty bad. We're outside Carmen's.*

Shit. The fighting had already started. *Is she going to be all right?*

I don't know, but she definitely can't fight, and there are at least five guys inside.

Ash's heart nearly stopped. *Where's Melody?*

These assholes are holding her hostage with Carmen and the kids. They say they're waiting for you.

Fuck. Ash changed direction and cut through the trees toward his sister's. Gregory was not only the oldest in the pack, he was also missing an arm. If he tried to fight, he was going to get himself killed. *Who else is with you?*

Just Brigit. The rest of the pack is on the other side of the pass hunting.

Ash lengthened his stride. He'd been so caught up in the financials, he hadn't thought to tell the pack he was leaving. Hadn't reminded them to stay close. He'd have to face Brennan's men with only Gregory to back him.

We need a bigger pack. His wolf whispered, swerving toward the creek.

Only as he neared the path to the old cabin did Ash realize where his wolf was taking him. *The squatters.* Would they come to his aid? Even if they did, it might not be enough.

His wolf insisted they try. Ash agreed.

Muscles burning and paws churning up snow, he dodged trees and vaulted bushes to reach the cabin near the creek. Ash shifted to human form without breaking his stride, crossing the small clearing to the cabin door. He pounded a fist on the thick wood. "Open up!"

The door opened a crack, and Matt took in Ash's nakedness in one sweeping glance. "Heard your howl. What's going on?"

Ash didn't have time for small talk. "You still want to join my pack?"

The man's eyes remained cold. "Your pack not answering you? That why you suddenly need my help?"

The woman's face appeared behind his shoulder. "What does it matter, Matt? We owe him for letting us stay here." She locked gazes with Ash. "How can we help?"

Ash hesitated, looking at the baby she clutched to her chest. He'd be putting this family in danger. But Brigit was already hurt, and without help, other members of his pack might die. *Melody might die.* "Another Alpha's holding my mate hostage, and most of my pack is away. I need backup."

Matt pulled the woman close to his side. "I'll join you, but only if you bring Trish into the pack, too."

Frustration growing, Ash clenched his fists. "You know humans can't be pack-bonded."

"Matt, just go." Trish nudged her mate forward. "Worry about me later."

"I'll take you both to the fucking glacier myself when this is over," Ash ground out. "But I need you to come with me *now*."

Matt grimaced, but at another nudge from his mate, he acquiesced and removed his shirt, revealing a scrawny chest laced with scars. The boy had been through some shit, but Ash didn't have time to question. Normally the bonding ritual was witnessed by the pack, but there was no time for ceremony.

Letting his claws emerge on one hand, Ash raked a set of shallow grooves over Matt's heart. Crimson blood welled up and flowed down his pale skin. Matt didn't even flinch, eyes fixed and bright as he watched Ash slice open his own hand.

Ash held up his bleeding palm. "Do you accept the bond of this pack, to protect and serve as your Alpha commands?"

"With honor."

Ash pressed his palm against the welts on Matt's chest, mingling their blood as he called on his Alpha power to bond them. Immediately, Matt's presence entered his head, joining the others. "Then accept the protection of this pack in return."

Far away, a chorus of howls split the air as the pack sensed the new member.

Ash swallowed back bile. He'd used his Alpha power more today than he had in almost a decade. His wolf was floating high and ready to fight, but he needed to be careful. Strategic. Even with Matt to help, he was at a disadvantage.

Ready? he asked Matt through the mental link.

Matt was already shifting, his body bowing into the shape of a russet wolf with light patches of fur matching his scars. *Let's go.*

As they pelted across the snow, Ash hoped that the young wolf was enough to tip the balance.

Melody stood in Carmen's living room, clutching her stomach. The baby hadn't moved since Brennan had knocked her from the machine, and she prayed it was all right.

Refusing to leave until he confronted Ash, Brennan paced the floor, picking up Carmen's things, looking at them, and tossing them aside. At least he'd found a pair of sweats; she was sick of watching him strut around naked, flaunting his massive erection like a badge.

His four betas were still in wolf form, following his movements with impassive eyes, but Melody knew they were poised to act the moment he commanded. They'd already proved they'd do anything he commanded, no matter how brutal. She shuddered, remembering poor Brigit's torn face and the blood spattered snow outside. They'd left the woman for dead, forcing their way past Carmen with Melody and Roxie in tow.

On the sofa, Carmen lay slumped on her side with her hands tied at her back, one eye swollen shut and blood dribbling from her broken lip. The children cowered on the floor beside her, Rory with an arm around each of his sisters.

"Let's just go," she begged. "I'll come without a fight. You don't need to hurt anyone else."

Brennan removed a family photo from the wall and cracked it against the corner of the entertainment center, shattering the glass so he could pull out the picture. He peered at the smiling faces. "I'm not leaving until I take down the man who thought he could steal my mate."

"Nobody stole me. I ran away. But I know better than that now." Melody swallowed her revulsion and moved closer to stroke his hairy chest in that simpering way he'd always liked. "Let's just go back to my grandfather and have the wedding."

Letting the photo flutter to the carpet, he grabbed her by the hair and jerked her head back, forcing her to bend her knees. "You think you're getting off that easy? You shamed me, Melody. You're a conniving little whore and need to be punished."

Clinging to his arm with both hands, she let a tear leak from the corner of her eye; he liked it when she cried. "Punish me, then. Take me home and make an example of me."

He flung her aside, sending her to her knees on the carpet. "I can't physically harm you. Not while you're carrying my heir." Turning his attention to Carmen and the children, he licked his lips. "But there are other ways to make you regret your choices."

"Please, no." Melody gulped. Her worst nightmare was at hand, and there was nothing she could do to stop it.

Carmen glared at Brennan through her one good eye. "My brother's done time for murder, but you can't even do your own dirty work. You have your wolves do it all for you. You think Ash'll hold back when it comes to kicking your whiny ass?"

"You want me to do my own dirty work?" Brennan raised a hand as if to strike, but froze as a howl outside rattled the windows.

An Alpha howl. It had to be Ash. Melody didn't know whether to be relieved or worried. She'd hoped to get Brennan out of here before he caused more bloodshed. Now the real fight would begin. People she cared about were going to get hurt or even die, and it was all her fault.

Brennan spun and signaled one of his men. "You, stay and watch that bitch and her brood. The rest of you, with me." Grabbing Melody's her, he hauled her back to her feet and pushed her toward the door. "My mate needs to watch me punish her lover so she never forgets what a real Alpha can do."

Her feet felt like lead as he shoved her into the mudroom. The baby felt heavy in her abdomen, pressing on her bladder. Now was not the time to need to pee. Unless… Brennan said he wouldn't hurt her while she carried his child. Could she use that to her advantage? She was barely six months along, but Brennan probably knew less about pregnancy and childbirth than she did.

Brennan opened the mud room door and pushed her through.

She stumbled forward, stopped sharply, and clutched her belly.

"What is it now?" Brennan growled.

She bent over and groaned. "I don't know. I think you'd better get me to a hospital."

He grabbed the hood of her coat and gave it a sharp jerk. "Do you think I'm an idiot?"

Keep it up. She groaned again, falling to her knees and breathing fast like she'd seen on TV. "It's too early. It can't come now."

He seized her face painfully with one hand, twisting her head to look at him. "You want to play this game? All right. I'll leave you here and bring along one of those pups to watch the carnage, instead."

Shit. She gulped a breath. "No, I think I'm fine. The baby must be reacting to my stress. Just give me a minute to get over the cramp."

With a huff, he stood, looming over her while she got back to her feet. "If you do anything like that again, I won't offer a second chance."

Gaze downcast, she nodded and moved to the outer door.

They stepped outside into the gray light of the oppressive clouds. She scanned the clearing, hoping to discover Ash had assembled an army, but found only three wolves lined up along the trees. She immediately recognized Ash's gray fur and gold eyes, and she was certain the three-legged wolf would be Gregory. The other reddish one she didn't know, but he looked small compared to Brennan's bodyguards.

In an instant, Brennan's wolves spread out to face them. Brennan pressed himself against her back, wrapping an arm intimately across her middle as he murmured in her ear, "If you move from this spot before I come for you, the bitch and her pups will suffer."

Ash's wolf shimmered, rising into the shape of a man. His face was hard, but concern lit his eyes. "Melody, are you all right?"

Melody nodded as Brennan moved past her, blocking her view.

"Talk to me, mongrel, not her!" Brennan barked.

"Fine. You're trespassing on Huntington territory," Ash said.

"I just came to retrieve my rightful property." Brennan tilted his head toward Melody. "And to remind my mate of her place."

"She's not your mate." Ash's eyes flashed.

Brennan grinned wickedly. "I was hoping you'd argue." In a blinding flash, he transformed and lunged forward.

His men joined his charge as if they'd known all along this was his plan.

Ash shifted just as quickly, a creature of long, sharp teeth and flashing eyes.

The two sides clashed in a flurry of snarls and fur, churning the snow with their paws. The small russet wolf yelped, going down under one of Brennan's betas, but wriggled free a moment later. Gregory had his teeth clamped on a beta's leg, refusing to let go even as the other wolf tore at his side.

Melody couldn't breathe. They were outnumbered, and the snow was growing red with blood. She had to do something. But what?

What sounded like a baby crying reached her and she spotted the woman from the cabin edging around the corner of the house. *What's she doing here?* The woman held a shotgun awkwardly against her shoulder and her baby in her other arm. No way could she hit what she was aiming at like that.

Keeping her eyes on Brennan's wolf, Melody edged toward her. "Here, let me."

The woman handed her the gun, biting her lip. "I only have one bullet."

Of course there's only one bullet. Melody nodded. "Then I'd better not miss."

Gregory now lay unmoving at the edge of the fight, leaving Ash to face three opponents on his own. Blood darkened her mate's gray ruff, and he snarled and slashed, trying to keep the wolves from flanking him. He lunged forward and sank his teeth into a red wolf's throat. They writhed over the crimson snow while Brennan's black wolf slashed at Ash's belly.

Shooting Brennan was impossible with so many wolves all close together. She needed to draw him away. *If I run, he'll chase me.* He wouldn't let her escape again. She took a few deep breaths and stepped into the clearing. Brennan had to notice her leave, and the best way to ensure that was to run directly across his line of sight.

"Stay behind the trees," she told the woman.

Making sure the safety was off, Melody grasped the rifle in both hands and bolted. She'd only have a few steps before he caught her and needed to be ready. She sprinted past the fray as if heading for the snowmobile shed, not bothering to see if Brennan followed. This was her only chance. It had to work.

Skidding to a stop, she pivoted, raising the shotgun at the same time.

Brennan had taken the bait and was nearly upon her. He leaped, bloodied fangs exposed in a snarl.

She didn't have time to aim, just pulled the trigger. The gun kicked. The black wolf flipped backward in the air. He landed in the snow in a shower of teeth and fur and blood. A growing pool of scarlet stained the snow beneath him.

Every wolf stopped dead in its tracks, as if holding their breaths.

In the silence, Brennan twitched once. Twice. Then lay still.

Ash released the wolf he had pinned to the ground and padded over to Melody. She put a hand on his ruff, digging her fingers into his fur. Her mind was reeling, and she thought she might throw up. *I just killed a man.*

But right now wasn't the time to show weakness. Sucking in a breath, she looked at Brennan's wolves and said in a surprisingly steady voice, "I suggest the rest of you leave before I pick another target."

Without protest, Brennan's remaining betas tucked tail and ran.

She watched them go, wondering how the pack she'd grown up in had become so corrupt. But that no longer mattered. She had a new pack, a new future. And for the first time, she was truly free to pursue her own path.

CHAPTER TWENTY-TWO

Sweat ran down Melody's forehead, and her spine felt like it was about to break. She'd heard childbirth hurt, but she'd never imagined experiencing this much agony. She wanted to die. "I need druuugs," she moaned.

Ash held her hand. "I love you," he murmured over and over.

She wanted to punch him, but this wasn't his fault.

The doctor in Anchorage said she was due in three weeks, and Ash had offered to fly her in and stay at a hotel last week. But they were short on funds, and she'd insisted the baby would wait until closer to her due date.

But this baby was coming tonight, right here in Ash's cabin.

"Push, Melody," Brigit said from the foot of the bed. "We're almost there."

Miraculously, not a single person had died in the fight with Brennan—other than Brennan himself. Brigit would carry a scar on her thigh and another at her temple, but both she and Gregory were as hearty as ever after a few weeks of healing. And it was a good thing, too, since Brigit was a midwife.

"I can't do it," Melody panted, rocking her head from side to side.

"You can," said Brigit. "You have to."

Another contraction clamped down on her, and Melody swore she was being split in half. Summoning all her energy, she pushed. And then, in a sudden gush, she was empty.

She sucked in a breath, surprised by how good it felt to finally be able to fill her lungs completely.

Brigit held up a wrinkled red infant with a shock of black hair. The baby wailed, small limbs flailing.

Ash kissed Melody's temple. "You did it! We have a daughter!"

But Melody was barely listening.

A rich, wordless presence she'd waited to feel her entire life was inside her head. A magic that slowly filled her body, from her scalp to her shoulders and chest, down her legs until even her toes tingled with energy.

Her wolf.

Hello?

The response felt like a doggy smile, all warm and loving. Wriggling with potential. With joy. More emotion than words, her wolf sent, *Our child.*

Tears filled Melody's eyes, and she looked down at the baby now lying on her chest, then at Ash looking into her eyes with such love and devotion.

"My wolf is here," she gasped.

He let out a breath. "I told you she was just waiting for the right moment. I can't wait to meet her, too."

A chorus of wolves began a howling song outside, welcoming her into the pack.

She pulled Ash down to kiss her.

Our mate. Her wolf panted with satisfaction.

Melody felt exactly the same way.

CHAPTER TWENTY-THREE

Ash stepped onto the dock to greet the mail plane. The fresh green scent of cottonwood sap filled the air, and the first tender spears of cattails had emerged along the shoreline. He was still on edge, waiting for retribution from Melody's old pack. But none had arrived so far, not even a request for Brennan's body.

He accepted the bundle of mail from the pilot and turned back toward the cabin, relieved there had been no passengers.

The Shifter Council had ruled Brennan's death an act of self-defense, and the black wolf's grave lay near the Quentin pack border, a warning to anyone thinking of encroaching on Huntington land. Matt and Trish had been accepted into the pack with open arms, and Carmen had even given the small family matching mukluks embroidered with beads. Ash had taken the couple to the glacier a few weeks ago, and Trish had been granted a wolf. Although the babies were far too young to play together, Melody enjoyed having another young mom as a friend.

As the mail plane buzzed back into the sky, Ash entered the forested the trail toward the house, flipping through envelopes, flyers, and assorted junk mail. A manilla envelope for Melody had arrived, along with a bill from the pediatrician. Melody no longer needed a doctor since she had her wolf to heal her, but they both felt better having the baby checked out.

A gray and brown wolf emerged from the brush, and Ash nodded a greeting to Yates. After the incident at the coffee shop, the man had spent a night in jail, but was released when Talvin declined to press charges. Turned out Yates had overheard one of the cops talking about an anonymous tip. Supposedly, a man with Ash's description was planning to murder someone, and Yates had realized Talvin's call was a setup. Ash would be forever grateful Yates had stepped in.

Yates shifted to human form and took up pace next to Ash. He looked at the envelopes in Ash's hands. "Anything for me?"

Ash handed him a flyer for a Memorial Day sale on furniture that was almost a week out of date. "Not unless you're the box holder."

"Damn, I wish I had a box to hold." Yates flipped open the flyer. "There aren't even any scantily clad women in these pictures. Any chance you're heading to Anchorage soon?"

Ash spotted a second past due notice on the mortgage and sighed. Reluctant to leave Melody to care for the newborn alone, he hadn't taken a job in almost a month, but he couldn't put it off any longer. "Yeah, I'll probably head out in the next day or two."

"Let me know so I can catch a ride. The ladies at the Bush Company are calling my name." With that, Yates shifted back to his wolf and loped off.

Ash let out a snort and continued on. After what Yates had done for him, the man could have free rides for life. Reaching the cabin, he kicked off his muddy shoes and headed inside.

Melody sat with her feet up on the sofa, dozing in front of another episode of Glee because the music soothed the baby, who now slept at her breast. Hearing him come in, Melody gently set the child in the basinet beside her and rose to greet him. "I've been waiting for you. She just fell asleep. Want to grab a little us time?"

His cock immediately jumped to life. Their sex life had been relegated to just a few quickies since the baby's arrival. Without another word, he swept her into his arms and carried her to the bedroom. She was already stripping out of her shirt as he set her feet on the floor, and he shucked out of his clothes as well, meeting her naked at the foot of the bed.

"God, I love these tits." He cupped Melody's heavy globes, running his thumbs over her hardening nipples.

Between the birth and the arrival of her wolf, her body had changed, become firmer and stronger, her breasts heavier. And she'd grown more dominant. Her wolf wasn't an Alpha, but it was strong-willed. It turned him on.

She pushed him back onto the bed and straddled him, running both hands down his front to his hips before bending to lick his chest. Her little teeth made his nipple harden, and he put his hands on her ass, flexing his hips up into her heat.

She moaned softly, rocking her slit along his length. Wetness coated him, and the scent of her arousal filled his senses.

Letting her do as she wished, he ran his palms over her soft skin, up her sides, cupping her breasts. Her nipples leaked a little milk, but he didn't mind. It was even a little sexy.

She lifted herself and put a hand between them, centering his head against her opening. When she sank slowly over him, he closed his eyes in bliss. She slid him in and out, rocking her hips with ever-growing urgency.

He gripped her ass, watching her throw her head back and ride him. She was so damn beautiful. He'd never imagined being this lucky.

Her inner walls fluttered, and she ground down against him with a moan. It took all his control not to come with her, but he didn't want this to end yet.

Giving her a moment to let the wave subside, he growled, "My turn," and flipped her onto her back.

Pinning her hands above her head, he looked into her passion-dark eyes and began filling her with sure, steady strokes. She panted, her heated core tightening as she thrashed her head from side to side. He captured her mouth in a kiss, savoring her sweetness as he pounded into her.

When she crested again, he was ready. Her pussy tightened around him, and she stifled a scream, wary of waking the baby. He buried himself deep in her heat, filling her with his seed.

Breathing hard, he pressed kisses along her neck, behind her ear. She stroked his back, legs wrapped around his waist as he slowly rocked them down from their bliss.

"You did good keeping quiet," she whispered.

He chuckled—she was the screamer, not him. "You didn't do too bad yourself."

"I'm hungry. How about you?"

He nodded and rolled off her. They cleaned up and dressed, tiptoeing by the basinet on their way to the kitchen. While he made them sandwiches, she sat at the counter and flipped through the mail. She held up an envelope. "Crap, another past due?"

He slid a plate with a turkey sandwich in her direction. "Yeah, I'm going to need to head in for a job tomorrow."

"I hate that." Her gaze fixed again on the bright red past due stamped on the envelope. "But I guess you have to."

"I'm sorry." He took a bite of his own sandwich. "Oh, there's a letter in there for you."

She pawed through and found the manila envelope. For a long moment, she stared at it without touching it.

"What is it?" he asked.

"It's from my grandfather's lawyer." He felt his hackles rise. Had the pack finally gotten around to pressing charges?

Pushing her plate to one side, she turned the envelope over and pried open the flap with shaking hands. For long moments, he watched her eyes move as she read, until he could bear it no more. "What does it say?"

"Grandfather's dead." She shook her head, a little furrow between her eyebrows, and handed him the packet. "As for the rest, you tell me."

Skimming the shifter legalese that would mean nothing in a human court of law, he realized it was the stipulations for her trust fund. He let out a low whistle when he saw the amount. Even he hadn't realized how much she'd stood to inherit, how much she'd given up to be with him. But when he reached the part about marriage requirements, he had to read it again.

From the living room, the baby fussed in the first stages of waking up. Melody went and got her, then sat back down at the counter.

Ash set the document between them. "If I'm reading this right, this says you'll inherit everything after you become an Alpha or marry one."

"Any Alpha, not just Brennan?" she gasped, eyes lighting with excitement. "You're an Alpha!"

He nodded. "Yes, I am."

This meant he wouldn't have to hunt any more bounties to pay off the mortgage. He wouldn't have to leave Melody alone. More than that, they could live in luxury for the rest of their lives.

Melody grinned and handed him the baby. "I think she needs a diaper change."

"So much for being an Alpha." Ash cradled the fussy baby against his chest and smiled, his chest filled with more joy than he even knew existed. Throw all the diaper changes in the world at him. He didn't mind. He had more than he ever dreamed of.

He was an Alpha who'd found his mate.

*D*ear Reader,

Did you enjoy Melody and Ash's story? Want more from me? If you enjoy unusual heroes and strong women who can tame them, you'll love my gargoyle in Sticks and Stones.

Sten has been hiding as a gargoyle ever since he crashed to earth hundreds of years ago. When someone offers to purchase the "statue" in Angie's garden, Sten knows he must flee—but can he leave behind the human woman he's protected since childhood and who's ultimately stolen his heart?

Tap the cover to get your copy now or keep reading for a sneak peek.

Thank you for reading!
Love, Tamsin

P.S. Be sure to check out all the Alaska Alphas books at https://books2read.com/rl/AuroraShifters

STICKS AND STONES
EXCERPT

$\mathcal{A}$ngie was up to her elbows in potting soil when a man's voice forced her to turn around. As the owner of one of Old Turnbull's historic houses, she was expected to be pleasant to tourists, even when they trespassed on what was clearly private property. She took a calming breath and pasted a smile in place. A man with salt and pepper hair and wearing an expensive business suit was running his palm along one of her life-sized gargoyle's wings.

"Can I help you, sir?" She didn't bother to brush her hands clean as she moved toward him. Tourists in the historic ghost town seemed to get more entitled every day, and while she appreciated the boost they created in the local economy, it sucked living in one of the most prominent landmarks.

"Just a moment, if you please." He didn't look at her, just moved closer to the statue, one polished shoe crushing the marigolds edging her garden bed.

The gargoyle had garnered more than its share of attention, but never as rudely as this. In the form of a perfectly sculpted man, at first glance it could be taken for a crouching Adonis with wings. But closer inspection revealed the wings to be more like a demon's than an angel's, with claws at the upper joints and tips. The figure also had small horns buried in the hair curling over his temples and a long tail tucked against the back of one leg. Angie wouldn't have been surprised if the statue's fisted hands had claws. Her father had once said it'd been guarding their family for generations. *If only it could defend itself against this creep right now.*

Scowling at the man crushing her heirloom flowers, she cleared her throat. "Sir? This is private property."

With obvious reluctance, he pulled his attention from the gargoyle and reached into his breast pocket, producing a business card. He held it out to her. "Winston York the Third, dealer in rare antiquities." As she accepted the card, his gray eyes flicked over her stained jeans and plaid button-down shirt. "I'm interested in purchasing your statue."

Without looking at the card, Angie pointed to the sign on the tall, wrought-iron fence surrounding her yard, hoping the guy would take a hint that he was unwelcome. "In case you didn't notice, this is a historic site. The statue belongs to the house."

"Then I'd like to buy the entire property." He turned his gaze to the Victorian style brick building with its covered wrap-around porch and small turret. The scrolled trim needed new paint and one of the windows on the upper level was still boarded up after a spring storm had dropped a tree against the house, but she'd been forced to funnel her limited funds into fixing the roof. Even so, it was in far better condition than the rest of Old Turnbull. Her home was no Frank Lloyd Wright, but the antiquities dealers and national historians always seemed to be knocking on her door.

York finished his perusal and arched a brow at her. "You are the owner, correct?"

That's it. She was done being polite; the ladies at the Historical Society could go jump in a lake. "I am. But I don't recall putting up a For Sale sign."

A condescending smile lifted the corners of his mouth. "Everything is for sale. How does ten percent over market value sound? I'll have an assessor here tomorrow."

Looking at York's slick suit and manicured fingernails, she was reminded of her father's stories about the mining town during the boom, when big investors had moved in to buy out all the little claims. The house was one of the few pieces of her heritage she'd managed to keep after her dad died.

Her chest grew tight thinking about her father, and she shifted her focus back to the moment. Just who did this York fellow think he was? The asshole hadn't even bothered to ask for her name.

Taking a step forward, she stood toe-to-toe with the man, eyes level with his. "This house is my home, Mr. York, not some fixer-upper for you to buy and flip. It's not for sale." She thrust the card back into his suit's breast pocket. "Now please remove yourself from my property."

His gaze dropped toward her chest. Great. If this guy turned full creepster on her, she was going to shove her garden trowel up his ass. But his focus lingered at the hollow of her throat where her mother's antique pendant hung.

She pulled her collar closed and stepped around York toward the gate, motioning for him to leave. "I have work to do, so please move along. I'm sure you'll find other things to interest you in town."

York narrowed his eyes, and her whole body tensed. She'd never been to a big city, but this was how she expected someone felt just before a mugger grabbed their stuff. Slowly, he readjusted the hem of his suit jacket. "My apologies if I've offended you, Miss—?" He stepped through the gate and paused on the cracked concrete that had once been a sidewalk, looking at her expectantly. "I'm afraid I didn't catch your name."

"You didn't ask." She pushed the gate closed, gritting her teeth against the nails-on-the-chalkboard screech. Getting the rusty hinges open again in the morning when she left for her shift at the diner was going to be interesting, but she wanted to make her point.

"Ahem, well, again, my apologies. I hope you will reconsider. I'll have my lawyer draw up papers and send them over. I'm sure you'll find my offer more than generous."

She met his gaze between the bars. "And I'm sure you'll find my refusal just as firm."

Turning on her heel, she stalked back to her pots, feeling as if her gargoyle's gaze followed her with pride.

Angie lay stiff beneath the covers, unsure if the sound she'd heard was a dream or her half-stray cat, Sally, getting rowdy with the dust bunnies. She was used to the creaks and groans of the old house, and usually slept like a rock, but she could swear she'd been woken by the awful sound of her gate hinges. Exhausted from a long day in the sun, she didn't want to get out of bed to check. The sound came again. Definitely the hinges. *Ugh. Was that York guy back to fondle her gargoyle?* The statue was too heavy to steal, but if that asshole was crushing more of her flowers, she might just shoot him.

Slipping from beneath the covers, she set her bare feet onto the chilly hardwood floor and tiptoed to the open window. The honey-almond scent from the bed of heirloom night phlox wafted in on the night breeze. Her bedroom was in the turret, its leaded glass panes overlooking the garden. She sometimes liked to just sit up here and admire her flower beds and the monstrous yet strangely sexy gargoyle that dominated the foliage.

She squinted over the shadows of flowers and leaves. The moon was a mere crescent hanging low in the sky, but she knew right where to look to see her gargoyle's broad shoulders.

The space there was empty. She rubbed her eyes, pressing her nose against the glass. Where was he? The darkness must be playing tricks on her.

A creak and a thud came from downstairs. She jumped, twisting away from the window and pressing herself into the heavy damask curtain. Was someone *inside*? Turnbull had zero crime, and she'd never worried much about locking up. They didn't even have a police station, relying on the county sheriff for the few incidents that arose. If she called 911, it might be an hour or more before someone arrived.

She tiptoed to the shelf where she kept her father's old rifle. Her father'd taught her to shoot from an early age, and the gun was loaded in case a bear or mountain lion decided to come sniffing around. She hadn't fired it since she'd purchased it back from the pawn shop a few years ago, and she hoped she didn't have to tonight; blood on her carpet and holes in her walls were the last thing she wanted.

Hoping to chase the intruder off, she moved down the narrow hallway to the stairwell and called, "Whoever's down there, I'm dialing 911."

Breaking glass tinkled in the parlor, and a man's voice said, "Oh, shit!"

Oh, hell no. What'd just broken? Maybe she'd rather shoot the bastard after all. She'd been buying back heirlooms as she could afford them and the few things she'd managed to acquire were precious. The sound of something heavy toppled below. "Fuck," she muttered. Clenching her teeth, she started down the stairs, not bothering with the lights. She knew every inch of this place, and right now, darkness was her friend. "You'd better leave now! I have a gun!"

She rounded the corner, heart in her throat. Against the dark backdrop of the parlor windows a huge silhouette of a man lunged toward her. Before she even thought about it, she fired, the stock slamming painfully against her shoulder and driving her backward. She'd forgotten what the kick of a rifle felt like, and the report left her ears ringing. Had she hit him? It took her a moment to reorient herself and bring the weapon back up. God, she hoped she didn't have to shoot a second time.

To her relief, the door to the porch wrenched open and whoever had been inside fled into the night.

"That's right, asshole!" She took a few steps after him but was forced to pause when her bare foot met broken pottery. Dammit, that better not be from her curio cabinet. She backtracked and flicked on the light switch.

The sight of her ransacked parlor was sickening, but that's not what froze her in place; across the collapsed remains of her Queen Anne sofa lay her gargoyle.

And he was getting blood on her carpet.

Get STICKS AND STONES and keep reading now!

Untamed Instinct

Bewitched Shifter

Midnight Heat

Wild Child

POST-APOCALYPTIC SCIENCE FICTION WRITTEN AS TAM LINSEY

Botanicaust

The Reaping Room

Doomseeds

Amarantox

ABOUT THE AUTHOR

Once upon a time I thought I wanted to be a biomedical engineer, but experimenting on lab rats doesn't always lead to happy endings. Now I blend my nerdy infatuation of science with character-driven romance and guaranteed happily-ever-afters. My monsters always find their mates, with feisty heroines, tortured heroes, and all the steamy trouble they can handle. I promise my stories will never leave you hanging (although you may still crave more!)

When I'm not writing, I'll be in the garden or the kitchen, exploring Alaska with my husband, or preparing for the zombie apocalypse. I also love wine and hard apple cider, am mediocre at crochet, and have the cutest 12-pound bunny named Abigail.

Interested in more about me? Join my VIP Club and get free books, notices, and other cool stuff!

www.tamsinley.com

facebook.com/AlaskaAlphas

bookbub.com/authors/aurora-shifters

amazon.com/author/aurorashifters